A WORLD WITHOUT EMOTIONS

EMILIANO FORINO PROCACCI

A WORLD WITHOUT EMOTIONS

This book is a work of fiction. The characters and places are products of the author's imagination. Any similarity to actual events, places or people, alive or dead, is purely coincidental.

Unstatus Luxury™
www.unstatusluxury.com

ISBN 978-0-578-83329-3

First Edition 2021
Second Edition 2022

To Melissa and Gabriele

My dear daughter, when you were born and I saw you for the first time, I realized how pointless it was to rush about trying to understand the universe. Often, by dint of looking far away, we can forget that the answer is here, now, around us; we just have to find the courage to look it in the eye.

Let the sun into your heart, express your art, give it shape, and send it out into the world, and it will bring you wonders in return.

I would recognize that smile of yours out of a million smiles, like the most beautiful flower opening on your face. The evening will come and you may feel more alone but think of me and make your life full

My dear son, I would like to take you to places you have never been, to teach you to appreciate the magic in a dewdrop, when the first light of a spring day tinges it with color as sunlight passes through it.

I used to think that one day I could reveal the secret of life to you, but I was wrong. The moment you came into the world, I realized that the secret of life is here.

Be strong, never give in to hate, respect others, love life and you will never have to regret missed opportunities as many do.

Dad

Table of Contents

CHAPTER ONE: FOLLOW YOUR STAR   11

1. The world in black and white   11
2. Drowning in the truth   28
3. Mirrored in a dream   45
4. Surprise in the eyes   57
5. The face of emotions   70
6. An explosion of emotions   83
7. As doves…   95

**CHAPTER TWO: THE BITTER AFTERTASTE OF
TRUTH**   112

1. Truth is a hallucination   112
2. The awakening   131
3. Like a secret Carbonari meeting   149
4. Revelations   159
5. Checkmate   167

CHAPTER THREE: THE EARTH'S BELLY   180

1. An unexpected journey   180
2. Jungle of emotions   197
3. Mask of smiles   208
4. Playing dice with emotions   232
5. The dichotomy of light and shadow   244
6. The field of poppies   261
7. The world in color   274

Author's note   290
Bibliography   301

CHAPTER ONE:

Follow Your Star

1. The world in black and white

In the vastness of the sky, clouds often gather so densely that light can barely pierce them. It is strange to think how this light, so fast and pure, must compromise in taking the form of lightning so it can spring from the darkness of the clouds and have an ephemeral life whose final echoes are lost in the distant clamor of thunder. Love at times seems to take the same path as light. Doesn't it seem as if it were born by chance in the hidden and solitary recesses of the heart? Like light, love races forth not fearing defeat, storming every defense, bewildering, thrilling and shaking up the entire existence of a human being, and then is lost in a distant rumble. These were the thoughts of Detective William Pattern as he gazed through dark eyes at the horizon, seeking inspiration to feel those strange sensations that were once called "emotions."

It was about to rain, but he didn't care and was happy to stay on the skyscraper's roof for hours. People described him as an eccentric because he dressed strangely. He usually wore a long black leather coat lined in red satin, with a black damask suit and vest peeking out with a red tie for a final touch of class that William never went without. His brown hair reached his shoulders and, though his superiors had often asked him to cut it, he had always refused. After all, in a world without emotions, such a thing couldn't make anyone angry. William's hand was wrapped in a white, blood-stained bandage and in it, he held a necklace with heart-shaped pendant with the letter "W" engraved in the center. The words he spoke were lost in the air, "Together, beyond the bounds of emotions."

Soon he would be arrested and sentenced to death; the sound of police sirens was disappearing into the leaden sky but would soon grow louder until the police were surrounding the skyscraper. A tear ran down his face, blending with the raindrops as if the sky were moved to compassion by the intensity of William's sadness and wanted to be part of his weeping.

How was it that our detective was one of the only people left in the world to feel emotions? Let's go back and try to understand the extraordinary events that had happened to a world full of people incapable of shedding tears or smiling.

William was born in Happiness City, a place like many others, maybe a little too quiet. Nothing much ever happened here, and the days followed one after the other, flat and monotonous. We could say midnight marked the end of one day and the beginning of the next, without creating the slightest ruffle of excitement. When William was a child, his grandfather Walter used to take him to the top of the hills just outside Happiness City to show him the constellations, and now and again a falling star would streak the night sky with its light, leaving behind the echo of the wishes of those watching it from the earth. Years later, though William was no longer a child, he still loved to greet his falling star in homage to his mother who had died many years ago. Her name was Madeline and she had passed away the day he came into the world. William's father had died in a car accident on his way back from the pharmacy where he had gone to buy medicine for his pregnant wife.

Grandfather Walter had taken care of the child, who was left an orphan, and just like the stroke of midnight when one day dies and another comes to life, the grandson came to fill his grandfather's heavy heart with pure life. His first wail burst into Walter's heart and turned into a beautiful song.

In Happiness City and every other city in the world, no one experienced emotions anymore. Everyone's faces were always completely expressionless. There were neighboring cities with odd names, almost like jokes, each named after an emotion. Rising on a hill, there was majestic Sadness City, surrounded by a high stone wall built by now-extinct ancient peoples. The fortification once served to defend the city from the attacks of barbarians who, back when the emotion of anger still existed among humans, would leave their lands to invade those of others to loot them.

On a plain with the placid River Lethe running through it stood Anger City, once the home of fearsome bandits but now a city like any other, full of people with impassive faces devoid of any sign of emotion. Further north were Contempt City and Disgust City, linked by a subway with a well-known tragic history, though these days no one would be pained to hear it. On the day that a new subway line opened between the two cities, a technical breakdown caused several cars to derail, killing many passengers. Though the incident was on the television news and images spread around the world, of course, no one shed a tear, not even the families of the victims. On social media, some called the catastrophic event "sad," but with no real sense of the meaning of the word. A little south of the other cities, on the banks of Lake Stinlia, was Fear City, and to the East, in evergreen woods was Surprise City.

From the day that emotions had left human beings, the world had changed, even the rules of communication were completely turned on their head. The number of burglaries and murders plummeted because people could no longer feel greed or the emotion of anger. At birth, infants were no longer welcomed with smiles and tears of joy, but by their mother's inscrutable expression as she tried in vain to calm their wailing. When these babies became teenagers and got a bad grade at school, they went home showing no trace of sadness. When they came to their parents, they were scolded with cold words that only distantly recalled the heated arguments that sometimes old people liked to reminisce about in the many bars dotted around the cities.

The movie theater was one of the places of entertainment that had now disappeared, and the memory of it had been lost to time. After all, there was no point in going to see a comedy, a love story or an adventure movie if you couldn't react by feeling emotions. At the end of the movie, no one would experience any kind of emotion inside, even for the briefest moment.

In the old days, you would hear children laugh and play because that's what they used to do to have fun and excitement. On Christmas Day and birthdays, they would give each other presents because giving and receiving gifts brought happiness. It was a custom that had vanished long ago from this world without emotions, where no one could feel the joy of unwrapping a present.

Casinos had been closed for years too because gambling had lost its appeal. The fear of losing a large sum of money, the elation of winning and the vague feeling of changing the course of events with a stroke of luck, were unknown in today's world. Restaurants weren't popular anymore because good food no longer gave people satisfaction. Even the most delicious dish seemed to have no taste. Walking along the city streets you could still smell the usual aromas of food, but they could no longer make a passerby's mouth water. It was as if the world had become a ghost, as if it had turned into a hazy reflection of what it had been and could no longer be.

William had lots of memories from his childhood. Once he had been to an amusement park, well known in the old days and now out of use, a place where children used to have fun. The rides stood still and falling apart. There was no music to lift the spirits, no one laughed or rough-housed. There were no children running around the place looking for a shiny candy apple or string licorice. This once magical fairground was now a museum where children were taken on school outings to learn about the "old world." Teachers would tell them how the world without emotions was perfect because there were no more wars, and human beings no longer committed atrocities against others or the environment. At school, they still studied the sublime works of the great poets of the past, but the children could only analyze the grammar because the words no longer seemed to inspire great gestures or crazy acts of love. No action was ever done in the name of love. No heart raced as the object of passion approached. There was no delight in conquering someone's heart, just as there were no tears when someone was left by the love of their life. The custom of bringing a woman a bunch of flowers was still alive, but it was more of a convention than a show of affection or an attempt to win her heart.

In a world without emotions, many once-crowded businesses were abandoned. When William was a child, he lived in a suburban neighborhood of Happiness City. Not far from his house was a huge abandoned building, surrounded by a high fence. Taking advantage of a hole in the fence, William and his school friends snuck into the building, where they found much of interest, not least a large phosphorescent sign saying "Bowling." William wasn't sure what people did there in the past, but it seemed to be a place for recreation. He and his friends often rolled the heavy bowling balls towards the pins, but none of them shouted for joy when they made a strike. The huge space also had plenty of dispensers, still full of candy and chocolate, but they didn't pique the children's curiosity in the least.

One day, young William was exploring the abandoned building when he heard a strange humming noise. Instinctively, he tried to find out where it was coming from, first peering behind a counter, then in the next room, but the humming seemed to come from somewhere else. Suddenly it got louder, turning into a metallic sound. If he had been capable of the emotion of fear, he definitely would have bolted out of there. But with a blank face and not a second's hesitation, he boldly went in search of the source of the noise. Full of curiosity and expectation, he pulled down hard on the handle of a door, which sprung open revealing the secrets hidden behind it.

The room was quite dark and a faint glow from a refrigerator with a glass front dimly lit the floor of tiles corroded by leaked rainwater. There was a pungent smell that would have appalled anyone in a world where the emotion of disgust still existed. The metallic sound was coming from the refrigerator, inside of which were shelves lined with ice cream packs of praline and cream, chocolate, apple and grape flavors. They must have been there for some time because on the packs was the image of a smiling child holding an ice cream cone. There was a time when such food would have brought an expression of happiness to a child's face.

William's grandfather had always told him about the beauty hidden in a smile, how once, when you showed your teeth and raised the sides of your mouth, you were sending a positive sign to others. Emotions had disappeared, but curiosity was still a distinctive characteristic of the young, so William opened the refrigerator and tried some of the ice cream by pushing his finger into a pack and then licking it. He started to cough because obviously the ice cream had been there some time and had by now long gone bad. Still, to emulate the child on the outside of the pack, he reached up to a nearby shelf, took a cone and filled it with handfuls of ice cream, after which he went up to a mirror and watched himself as he smiled just like the child on the pack. It was getting late, and he had to go home but exploring the old world hadn't yet satisfied his thirst for knowledge. So it was at that very moment that he decided to be an explorer when he grew up. He wanted to travel and find out why some places that were once the center of people's lives were now only relics buried under the gray blanket of time.

But, life, we all know, rarely goes as intended and has a habit of upsetting future plans. The years passed, and William did not become an explorer; he enrolled at the police academy to train to be a detective. All the students could choose their field of specialization at the academy and he chose psychology. He had always been curious and wanted to understand the mental mechanisms behind human actions. At first, he wasn't sure he wanted a career in the police force, but his grandfather urged him to go for a job that would give him a steady salary. Besides, the job didn't involve much risk, according to statistics there was very little crime, and it had been years since a police officer had been killed on duty. Drugs used to kill people, but now they had almost disappeared from the market because they no longer brought people a sensation of intense wellbeing that caused addiction. Even the underworld had closed up shop because there was no more hate in the world and no desire to get rich.

1.1

During his years at the academy, William studied and led a seemingly normal life, but on the weekend, to satisfy his love of exploring new places, he visited the old world. One fine spring day, he decided to visit a ghost city by the name of Calicraston Ville, abandoned long ago in the days of the gold rush. To get there he had to take the highway to an intersection with a little-used, dusty, country road. That day an unexpected event would change his life forever.

After following the road for a few miles without meeting a soul, he stopped the car in front of a rusty iron gate from which hung a yellow sign: "Sequestered Property." Like the rearguard of a defeated army, the sign was still there doing its duty by warning the rare visitors. William climbed over the gate and headed for a crumbling rectangular building, on whose weather-beaten walls you could still make out the faded shapes of some musical notes. The building had once been the recording studio where some of the world's most famous singers recorded their albums. From the moment emotions had left human beings, music dropped in popularity because no one could understand its meaning anymore. A good song no longer made the hearts of young couples leap as they gazed into each other's eyes, exchanging silent vows of love.

William walked around the building looking for a point of entry until he found an open window. Clearly, someone had been to that lonely place before him. Once through the window, he found himself in a darkish room. There was a thick layer of dust on everything, but it was all in order. There was even a desk in fine wood on which there still lay a pen with one of those colored pads for writing memos. It seemed as though the occupants had left the place in a hurry, possibly to escape something terrible. The telephone was in its place on the desk, as was the computer and gold vinyl records lined up on a shelf. Hanging on the wall was a portrait of a quite heavyset person wearing a crown and holding a microphone.

William noticed something strange in a dark corner of the room. Hesitantly, he walked over until he could make out some gold ingots displayed on a shelf. In all likelihood, this was loot left there by someone when gold was still valuable. A long time ago gold had been precious, used to make jewelry. Now it was a metal like any other, maybe even the humblest of them all, precisely because no one gave presents made of gold anymore. Since the feeling of love was emptied of emotion, everything had changed. Now gold was no longer used to make wedding rings but for hubcaps. Sometimes the hubcaps would come loose on moving cars, rolling into the gutter at the roadside, and since they were shaped like a bowl, the homeless would pick them up and use them to beg with.

Just then, William had a hallucination: the room around him turned into a beautiful garden full of colored flowers. You could hear the gurgle of a small brook, while pairs of little chattering birds chased each other. On a bench was a young woman with long honey-colored hair and eyes like the deep sea who was reading a book. She wore a long pink dress and around her neck hung a heart-shaped pendant with the letter "W" engraved in the center. The sun was about to go down behind the horizon, but somehow it seemed to hesitate as if it would like to bathe the young woman's face a moment longer with its gentle rays. She looked up from her book and turned to William. He experienced a peculiar sensation, a sort of heart pang, but before he realized what was happening, the illusion suddenly disappeared. He returned to himself and shook his head, rubbing his eyes. Maybe exhaustion was making him hallucinate, but the images were so vivid and real.

He had to carry on with his exploration because the sun would soon set, and William didn't want to still be in that building in the dark. Though he didn't know fear, if someone had attacked him, as often happened in the old world where anger was a common emotion among people, he would have to defend himself. Picking up a silver paperweight from the desk, he switched on his flashlight and began to hurry along a corridor so dark it could greedily swallow his dim light struggling not to get caught in the thin weave of darkness.

At the end, the corridor opened into a great atrium invaded by wild climbing plants and towered over by a glass ceiling through which the light filtered. A loud metallic noise coming from the floor above made William jump, and without stopping to think, he ran up the stairs until he reached a metal door locked with a chain and a large padlock bearing a strange symbol. It was a triangle enclosed in a circle inside which were two crossed swords beneath the initials "M" and "C."

Bam! The metallic sound rang out again and seemed to be coming from the room behind the door. William picked up an old fire extinguisher in the corner and delivering several well-aimed and decisive blows, he broke the chain. The origin of the metallic noise wasn't yet clear. Suddenly, out of nowhere, a large wild boar followed by her young, barged past him, propelling him to the floor. The animals kept on running, vanishing into the darkness.

In the room was an electric panel with a large lever in the center that could be lifted to turn the power on throughout the building. Down in the hall, classical music was playing and a large decorative ball hanging from the glass ceiling on a steel cord, began to spin causing the dust collected on top to waft around.

William hurried back downstairs and on down a corridor linking a series of rooms to the managerial offices, inside of which were more desks, computers, chairs and bookshelves. At the end of the corridor was another door locked by a padlock with the same symbol as before, the triangle enclosed in a circle inside which were two crossed swords beneath the initials "M" and "C." He had no idea what was behind the door, but if music somehow used to arouse emotions in human beings, maybe he would find the answers there to satisfy his innate curiosity. Again, he picked up an extinguisher, broke the padlock and pushed the door open. The sight inside left him speechless.

There was a slow-rhythm melody playing in the room, very much like a lullaby. Most of the plaster from the walls had fallen to the floor; in a corner were some dust-covered computers and electronic equipment. Between an old reel-to-reel projector sitting on a table and a large white screen on the wall, many chairs were in a row, and occupying each chair was a skeleton. William went to have a closer look. They must all have stopped breathing while watching the screen and seemed totally unaware that death was so close. Each skeleton wore a blue jumpsuit with a little cloth patch showing the flags of different countries. A piece of yellowed paper was sticking out of the breast pocket of a jumpsuit on which the name patch said "Mike." William slowly extracted it, without feeling the slightest disgust or fear, and read the following:

> Dear Mike, I was followed. They have discovered the resistance's hiding place and confiscated all our promotional material. We need to find another printshop to make more flyers. The new slogan is, "The cure is in

emotions. Don't be made to conform." We must be careful because Minedal-e Corporation has spies everywhere. I hate the witch at the head of that organization. If I could, I would kill her with my own hands! In the remote possibility that I make it, we'll meet at the recording studio in three days. I miss you and cannot bear being apart. This handful of words written in ink and tears cannot begin to express what I feel right now. I love you.

Your Jacqueline

You didn't need to be a detective to realize that the initials "M" and "C" engraved on the door padlocks in the building stood for Minedal-e Corporation. Who was at the head of it?

Jacqueline was clearly a member of a sort of resistance organization. Strangely, her message written on the yellowing piece of paper showed that she felt emotions. Had Jacqueline really felt love, or had she written, "I love you" purely out of convention? What were the remains of the resistance members doing there? The answers to these questions could not be found, at least not yet.

William switched on the old reel-to-reel projector and after a brief squeaking noise, it started to project images onto the screen. There was no sound, but you could clearly see people smiling, some of them dressed in clothes that had been out of fashion for ages. Children were playing cheerfully on the swings in a park, smiling happily. Their parents were holding them tenderly in their arms. A child fell off the swing, and for some reason that William couldn't understand, water began to appear from the child's eyes. They were tears caused by the pain that only a parent can soothe. Then words appeared on the screen like a commercial, and even though the quality of the image had been drastically compromised, you could read fragments of the following message: "They are robbing us... we've got the cure... join us in the fight against Minedal-e Corporation!" Then "Emosemvi" appeared on the screen alongside a white mask like the ones used in the theater, with three red tears just below the holes for the eyes. The images stopped and the projector automatically turned off.

That place must have been the general headquarters for the resistance organization Emosemvi. Somehow its members were found and killed by the armed wing of Minedal-e Corporation. It all seemed so absurd. More investigation was needed. William had the feeling that he was being watched and decided to leave.

He thought that he should go straight to the academy, find his superior and tell him that he had found the skeletons. But that would mean explaining why he was there in the first place and, especially, why he had entered a building that had been sequestered by the authorities. The best thing to do would be to go back to the academy and not speak to anyone about his discovery, or maybe just confide something to his classmate Leonardo.

He went up to a dusty desk in the corner of the room, on which lay a pen with a red plastic rose attached to the end. Those poor skeletons had never had a proper burial; a flower, even a plastic one, would pay them some kind of tribute. At that point, he did something unusual but instinctive and put the red rose in the buttonhole of the skeleton's jumpsuit with "Mike" written on the patch. It wasn't clear whether these were the remains of members of a terrorist organization, but William felt the need to show respect for the death that had taken them by surprise.

Meanwhile, it was getting late and the sun was disappearing to make room in the sky for the moon. When he reached his car, which he had left parked in front of the gate just outside the building, he noticed fresh tire marks on the dirt path. Someone had followed him, confirming his feeling that he had been being watched when he was in the recording studio.

2. Drowning in the truth

Six months after the bizarre discovery of the skeletons at the recording studio, William completed his course at the academy. The swearing in ceremony was very solemn, all the recruits were lined up in the central courtyard and while their families watched from the bleachers, the chief of police made a speech wishing them all good luck. The recruits hadn't seen their families for months, and yet at the end of the ceremony, they simply shook hands with their parents in a mechanical manner. No joy appeared on anyone's face, no one exchanged a hug. William didn't have family to greet because Walter, his grandfather, had died a few years earlier from a degenerative illness. On the day of his funeral, the church had been packed with people and his coffin was placed up by the altar. At the end of the service, those present had come up to shake William's hand and to speak with indifference of things of little matter.

Religious gatherings were rare, only a distant reminiscence of a vanished society, like an echo of a voice lost in time. All types of religion had ceased to exist because humans no longer feared death, let alone the judgment of God. There was no joy to be felt in giving something, so even gratitude had disappeared. The lack of emotions had somehow repressed most sentiments as well.

At the end of the ceremony at the academy, William went back to his dormitory to collect his things and take them to the apartment in central Happiness City he had inherited from his grandfather. Over the last six months, he had put aside the discovery of the abandoned recording studio because he was too busy studying to finish his program at the academy. Leonardo, his classmate, joined him. He was the only person he had confided in about the skeletons in the abandoned building, "It's finally over. Are you happy, William?"

"What do you mean?"

"I don't know. My parents always ask me if I'm happy, and I say I am. It must be something positive. I'm going to do a placement shadowing an experienced detective and then I'm going to specialize in hostage negotiation."

"But Leo, does anyone actually take people hostage anymore?"

"Well… no, but you never know, anything could happen, and we've got to be ready. You've specialized in psychology, there'll definitely be a job for you at the department in Sadness City. Why don't you come with me?"

"No, I'm going back to Happiness City. I grew up there, and I know I'm doing the right thing."

Leonardo neared William and whispered quickly, "Listen… my father knows this bigwig in Sadness City. If you like, I can help you with your career, but you have to come with me."

William stood looking at his friend for a moment before replying. Leonardo was thickset, with curly hair that had a coppery tinge, a thin nose and large glasses that made him look like an aging math student. In some ways, he was physically very similar to his father. If he went with him, it would mean a step up in his career. If William were able to experience emotions, he would have thanked him and probably given him a warm hug of gratitude, but nothing of the sort happened. He simply said, "Thanks, but I'd rather follow my own path. We'll stay in touch."

"I don't think you're doing the right thing, but OK. See you later" Leonardo said coldly before walking out.

While William finished packing his bag, he stopped to re-read the letter he had found a few months before in the pocket of the skeleton's jumpsuit at the dilapidated recording studio. Who was this Jacqueline who had written the letter? One thing was for sure, the skeleton in whose pocket he found the letter must be that of a certain Mike, and Jacqueline loved him.

He put the letter back in a green folder, headed for the door and left for home.

During the night he had a strange dream. He was talking with a blond woman sitting on a bench. "I like my mess. There should be a bit less order in the world. Order is useful to keep things balanced, but isn't that just a paradox?" She was holding a pendant in her hands. Then she moved closer and whispered sweetly in his ear, "Open your eyes. The world is not as you see it." William opened his eyes and woke with a start. It was the same woman as the one in the strange hallucination he had had in the recording studio. He was sure of it.

Lulled by the images in the dream, he quickly fell back asleep. The next morning, he was woken by the sound of thunder, the alarm clock on his bedside table showed 10:00 a.m. and outside it was raining. It took him a while to recall the events of the previous evening, but then he remembered getting home and drinking a half glass of red wine to celebrate the end of his program at the academy. He had a monumental headache and only just managed to get up and go to the bathroom, where he washed his face and headed for the kitchen to get some breakfast.

As he drank a glass of milk for breakfast, he found himself looking confused at the kitchen table. There were his car keys and wallet, but something was missing. He couldn't immediately think what it was, but then, as if someone had suddenly thrown a glass of water at him, he leapt up from his chair. The previous evening, as he came in, he had left his keys, wallet and the green folder containing Mike's letter from the mysterious Jacqueline on the table. It couldn't have just disappeared into thin air unless, of course, someone had snuck into his apartment during the night! But who could possibly have known about the existence of that letter? Why would a thief steal the green folder and not his wallet? There was something weird going on, and he would have to find out what, but first he had to think of his safety, so he went to get his service pistol and loaded it. While a thousand thoughts were racing around his brain, the ring of the phone brought him back to reality. A police officer was calling to ask him to present himself at Happiness City police station and meet his new boss, Chief of Police McMillan.

He reached the police station's underground parking lot and after giving his identification number to the officer on the gate, he parked and then headed up to the main hall. Here an officer by the name of Stuart welcomed him with the words, "Hey, rookie. You here to meet the chief?"

"Yes, do we know each other?"

"OK, take it easy, William. You can smell the academy a mile off. Am I wrong?"

"No, you're right, but how do you know my name if we've never met before?"

Stuart was maybe not expecting that question and seemed somewhat disoriented. He took an audible breath and replied, "It's a small world. Anyhow, fill in this form and then follow me. I'll show you around the station and then you can meet McMillan."

Officer Stuart was like a character out of a comic strip, on the tall side but with short arms. An oval face framed pronounced features and he had a large mustache with the ends thinned and curled upwards that gave him a strange look. He rarely acknowledged people and was rude to anyone he did speak to because he was about to retire and had no interest in nurturing interpersonal relations, considering them a waste of time and energy.

William filled in the form and then he and Stuart set out on a tour of the headquarters. The police station had been renovated recently and included an Olympic swimming pool, a firing range, briefing rooms and a recording studio to make national television and radio announcements on air in the case of a natural disaster or other emergency. Then Stuart led the way down a long corridor to a large room full of police officers sitting at desks. For privacy, each workstation was located in a cubicle surrounded on all sides by black plastic panels.

"You're looking at our intelligence center and since you put on the form that you have specialized in psychology, this is the place for you. It's the hub of operations planning," said Stuart.

"We'll see, for now, I just need to meet the chief."

"Perhaps I'm not being clear. You don't choose what you do in this place. Anyways, you'll soon learn how things work."

Stuart opened a wooden door and inside, sitting behind a desk on which lay scattered piles of loose-leaf paper, was the chief of police, Richard McMillan. Not a very tall man, he was noticeably overweight and had jet black hair. With his small dark eyes and inquisitive stare, he managed to intimidate everyone he met. Addressing Stuart, he said, "How many times have I told you to knock before entering my office?"

"Yes, sir, sorry, sir. I've brought the rookie to see you. Will is fresh out of the academy and specialized in psychology."

"You're the one who needs a psychologist, Stuart. Get back to work!"

"Good morning, sir. My name is Pattern, William Pattern."

"Sit down, son."

Meanwhile, Stuart left the room, closing the door behind him.

"So, William, what do you expect from this job?"

"I expect to serve my country, sir."

"Yeah, that is what they teach you to say at the academy. It's not wrong, but repeating a phrase from memory doesn't mean you have really understood its meaning, don't you agree? Anyway, first you must cut your teeth on street patrol and, if you do a good job, you can have a desk in this department. There aren't many criminals, but bad things can always happen."

As he listened to what the chief of police had to say, William's eyes wandered to a wall hung with commemorative awards. One of them caught his attention. In large print, it read, "For the invaluable contribution of Chief of Police McMillan to Minedal-e Corporation."

"William, do you understand what I am saying? Are you day-dreaming, son?"

"No, no, it's all clear. I was just looking at all your certificates and awards, certainly for the excellent work you've done, sir."

"Right. Starting from tomorrow you are on car patrol to get some experience. You may go."

"Yes, sir, thank you, sir. Just one thing. When I was at the academy there was a rumor about an abandoned recording studio. They say there were skeletons in there. I was wondering if you had ever heard anything about it or if it is only a story."

"I don't think we've ever received a report of such a thing. Where is it?" asked the chief of police.

"It's not far from the academy. You take the highway north and then turn onto a country road. It's near Calicraston Ville, the abandoned town."

"Ah, I know the place, in the middle of nowhere. I can't send men out there without a good reason, but I'll tell you what, I will have someone look into it and if they find anything interesting, I'll let you know, OK? Now, off you go because I've got a press conference in a moment."

As William left the room his mind was bursting with questions he found it hard to answer, so he decided to go home and do some thinking.

2.1

As soon as he got home, he turned on the computer and did an internet search on Minedal-e Corporation. It was a pharmaceutical company with branches all over the world, one of which was located in the countryside not far from Disgust City. The president of the corporation was a certain David Shelton Malthen, son of the famed infectious disease expert, Paul Shelton Malthen. The latter had received great recognition from the scientific community for his contribution to research into creating a vaccine to combat Coris-91, a powerful virus that had spread across the world in the past, reducing the world population by 35%. It was a dark page in the history of humanity. The virus was transmitted by air, so people had to wear masks and keep a distance of at least six feet from others. The world was hit by a terrible economic crisis and even food began to run out; the virus was so lethal that it killed with alarming speed. The streets were full of corpses and the security forces were so hard put to bury them that mass graves were created. The world seemed to be a step from extinction, but then Dr. Paul Shelton Malthen discovered a cure for the virus, created a vaccine and saved humanity.

At this point, William was trying to figure out how a pharmaceutical company could impound a recording studio, the one where he had found the skeletons, and why it would do such a thing. Maybe he should just turn up at the local branch of Minedal-e and ask questions.

He had been sitting in front of the computer for a long time and hadn't realized that he'd totally forgotten to eat dinner. By now, it was dark outside and through the pouring rain, he could hear the roar of thunder echoing across the sky and rattling the windows. Suddenly, there was a knock at the door. William didn't feel in danger but nonetheless, just as a precaution, he grabbed his pistol and put it in the large back pocket of his pants. He opened the door and stood there speechless. An athletic-looking woman was standing in front of him holding out a cake. She wasn't just any woman, but the one who had appeared in the hallucination and in his dream; her long honey-colored hair was loose and fell to the shoulders of the long pink dress. She was the first to speak, "Hi, my name is Beatrice Whites. I'm your new neighbor, and I've just moved in."

William was staring at her and couldn't summon a word. The woman's delicate features were matched by the clarity of her eyes, lighting up her face.

"I've made a cake for each of my new neighbors, and this one is for you."

He still couldn't get a word out, so Beatrice pressed him, "If you don't want it, I'll eat it."

"No. Thank you!" he answered.

"So you don't want it?"

"No… I mean, yes, thank you, of course, I do. Why not come in for a moment? I was just about to eat," said William.

"Thanks, but mommy told me never to trust strangers."

William shook his head. He wasn't sure he knew quite what she meant by her reply.

"Come on, I was just joking. I can't right now because I've got to finish taking the cakes around."

"Joking? So you know what the word means? I mean, you know what a joke is?"

"Yes, I read it in a book. People would make a joke to provoke a reaction in the person they were speaking to."

"Yes, exactly. Are you a teacher?" asked William, curious.

"No, I'm a restorer. I restore antique furniture and works of art. How about you?"

"I'm in the police."

"Interesting. But I have to go. It was nice to meet you, Mr.… what's your name?"

"William, my name's William."

The woman placed the cake in his hands and disappeared around the corner of the landing. It wasn't unusual to get a visit from a new neighbor, but this neighbor was also the person featured in his hallucination and his dream. It couldn't be a coincidence. William hadn't noticed whether the woman was wearing the heart-shaped pendant, but there would be time for that. He felt strangely attracted to her and would have done anything to see her again. Too many strange things were happening in his life.

He closed the door and made some soup for dinner and then went into the living room to lie on the couch. With his head still full of questions, he let his eyes wander around the room. There was a large marble fireplace with the mantelpiece held up by a pair of statues. On one wall, in pride of place, was a painting of a bucolic landscape, while another wall was almost entirely taken up by shelves full of books, with a bronze ladder to reach the top ones. One book seemed to be sticking out further than the others, William went up to push it back in, but it wouldn't go, so he pulled the book out and realized there was something behind it. He stuck his hand in and pulled out a small videocassette. He didn't remember having seen it before; maybe his grandfather had left it there for some reason. He put the book back on the shelf and inserted the videocassette into the video player connected to the big television in the living room.

Images began to roll. It seemed to be a film taken during a wedding. In the old days, on such occasions the most frequent expression on people's faces was that of happiness, but in the video, the blankness on most faces left little room for doubt. The video showed the young couple as they welcomed their relatives. The bride's mother came up, shook her by the hand, and with a wooden expression said, "Good job. This is a good achievement."

"Thank you, now our new life begins."

Her father came up too, asking, "Will you go on a honeymoon now?"

"Yes, we're going to a resort in Disgust City."

Then the scene is interrupted by another in which the couple is cutting the wedding cake. Many people are clapping around them, but as can be imagined, there are no smiles. William hadn't recognized anyone who appeared on the video until he suddenly jumped to his feet exclaiming, "Mom!" The cameraman had zoomed the lens to frame Madeline, William's mother, asking her what she thought of the wedding, and she replied, "I wish Tom and Lara all the best. Today we are celebrating love. Look how sweet they are." The cameraman moved the video camera to the left to film the couple again as, with icy faces, they were welcoming the guests. Meanwhile the photographer took stills of the couple in a series of poses but with their expressions remaining strictly neutral.

William had never before seen his mother in a video; come to think of it, he only had two pictures of her. Then again, he had no pictures of his father at all and didn't even know what he looked like. He rewound the tape back to see the scene where his mother was talking with the cameraman when something unexpected happened. At the point when the cameraman first turned the video camera towards Madeline, she smiled, immediately afterwards, assuming a neutral facial expression. William rewound the tape again and then put it in slow motion. There was no doubt about it, for a second, his mother had smiled. This couldn't be possible and yet the images seemed clear enough.

The coils of the night encircled the world and silence whispered a lullaby into William's ear, sending him to sleep on the couch, while the still image of Madeline's face was fixed on the television screen.

The sharp trill of his cell phone echoed around the room. He answered with a drowsy voice, "Yes?"

"It's Stuart from the police station. What's happened to you?"

"Why? What time is it?" asked William, confused.

"That's a good start. It's eight o'clock on your first day at work. Aren't you coming in? John Apate, your patrol chief, is here waiting. Get a move on!"

"Yeah, I'll be right there."

William stood there for a minute longer, gazing at the sight of his mother's face on the television. Then he quickly showered, dressed, drank a glass of milk and left. All the officers who did not enter the force through a competitive exam wore a uniform, but those who had graduated from the academy could wear any type of civilian dress, as long as they wore the identification badge at the neck or belt. William could, therefore, continue to wear his eccentric damask outfit, which showed off his lean, muscular physique, and his long black leather coat lined in red satin.

Waiting for him when he got to the police station were Stuart and John Apate, the head of the patrol he would be working in. Apate was tall and broad with thin hair and chestnut eyes; his severe features and a restless expression suggested a determined personality. "Now, Mr. Pattern, let me make one thing clear. I teach you how to work on the beat, and you do as I tell you. First off: do not be late for work."

"OK, John, I don't know what happened to me today. I'm usually very punctual. It's all understood."

"Though you still have the smell of the academy on you, at least try to show some humility, and you'll get off on the right foot. And I suggest you cut your hair."

"I'll bear it in mind, John. Thank you for the advice."

"Right, it's late, so we had better be off."

They got in the car with John at the wheel. He was a resolute type with rough manners.

Happiness City was a peaceful place and seen from the inside of a police car it seemed even more so. John was the first to speak, "In this world, romantic relationships begin apathetically. No smiling or winking, and they end in exactly the same way. You know that already, don't you? But I'm not interested in how the world goes. Do you know why?"

"Why?" asked William.

"It was obviously a rhetorical question. You didn't need to answer. What I meant was that the world doesn't interest me because I've got whisky, a cure-all that solves problems. Its greatest quality is that it keeps me company in silence and doesn't ask questions."

William didn't reply. The guy was surly but basically seemed a good person. First stop was a stadium, where they showed their badges to the security guards at the gates and parked the car. Then John said, "Now, there is an important soccer game going on inside. We're not here to enjoy the match but to catch emozifledrin dealers. It's not a drug, just a sort of medicine that can, they say, give the taker strong emotions. Of course, that's bullshit, but there are people who buy and sell it illegally."

By now they had reached the steps up to the bleachers. William had never been to the stadium before and had no idea how many people it could hold. "There must not be many spectators inside because there is barely a jumbled buzz of voices," he thought.

When he got up to the bleachers, he couldn't believe his eyes: the stadium was packed with fans. No one shouted or sang at the top of their voice. Everyone sat in their seat in an orderly fashion and seemed unlikely to stand other than to go to the restroom. Following a goal, one of the spectators, without showing energy or enthusiasm, said, "It's in the net, now it will be easier to win the game."

A man with a black hat and long beard furtively passed a small plastic bag to the person sitting next to him. John went closer, but no sooner had the man see him than he leapt to his feet and began to run down the stairs. John darted after him and William did the same, running as fast as possible. In the meantime, the dealer had reached the parking lot and was trying to get in his car, but William managed to grab him by the jacket and pull him down to the ground. John came running up and quickly pulled out a pair of handcuffs to put on the dealer's wrists. They found several doses of emozifledrin in his jacket. John congratulated his colleague, and then he turned to the dealer and started to read him his rights.

The dealer, who was tall and muscular, reacted placidly. With no trace of anger, he said, "I ran away because I don't want to end up in jail. Living in the open air, free to choose what to do every day is better... I mean I'd rather that."

John helped the dealer into the back of the police car, shut the door and got into the driver's seat.

As William got in, he said to his colleague, "You deserve all the credit. I hadn't even noticed what the man was doing."

"You'll eventually get an eye for it. Anyway, not bad for a first day's work!"

"Yeah, though that guy didn't put up much of a fight. He's physically twice our size!" marveled William.

"No one overreacts to arrest because anger and fear aren't involved anymore," replied John coldly.

"That's true. There's no trace of it even in our hearts."

John was silent and started the ignition. They set off for the police station, where there was a cell waiting for the dealer.

3. Mirrored in a dream

William was walking up the stairs of his building with thoughts of the dealer's arrest still bubbling in his head. On the landing he ran into Beatrice, who was carrying a large bowl and nodded briefly to him. She was probably in a hurry or just didn't feel like talking. Glancing at the folds of her white shirt, he noticed she wore a heart-shaped pendant, exactly like the one belonging to the woman in his hallucination. Who was she really? They had first met recently when she had knocked on his door with the cake, but long before she had appeared in that strange hallucination at the recording studio.

While he was trying to figure it out, he reached the front door of his apartment and found it ajar. "Someone must have gotten inside! Maybe even whoever stole the green folder with the letter from Jacqueline," he thought, his gun in hand as he went in. The place had been turned upside down. Books were scattered everywhere, as were his clothes and other personal effects. Then his bedroom door made a creaking noise as if someone were trying to close it. William rushed over, kicked it open and saw a man standing in the middle of the room. His finger was on the trigger ready to shoot when he recognized his friend from the academy. "Leonardo! What are you doing here?"

"I came by to see you, but when I got here the door was open and a tornado seemed to have hit the area."

"Leo, weird things are going on in my life. Let's have a drink, and then I'll go ahead and file a report at the police station."

Leonardo helped him tidy the place; strangely, the thief didn't seem to have taken anything. Perhaps they had heard Leonardo coming, and in their hurry to leave, hadn't managed to grab anything of value.

William and Leonardo spent the evening together, reminiscing about times at the academy and telling each other about their new jobs in the police force. Remembering a shared moment with someone would have provoked a rush of emotion in the old days, but now it didn't have the same effect. The conversation between the two friends was monotonous:

"Do you remember the time Sergeant Garden asked you to shave your beard because you looked like a bush? And you answered, 'Yes, Sergeant Gardener!'" said William.

"Yes, of course. And do you remember when you were on dormitory cleaning duty and you overdid it with the floor polish? The Colonel slipped around the place as if he were dancing a jig."

"Yeah, I remember."

"The Colonel died recently of a heart attack," added Leonardo in an indifferent tone.

"I didn't know that."

After downing his last drop of beer, Leonardo said goodbye to William, promising to call him soon so they could go out together again.

William checked all the rooms in the apartment, even opening the closet in his bedroom to be sure no thieves were hiding inside. He had a huge headache, so he went to lie down and immediately fell into the arms of Morpheus.

He opened his eyes, but the room around him didn't appear to be his, even the furniture was different. Sunlight filtered through a large window and brushed the legs of his grandfather Walter who was sitting in a rocking chair, with a smiling face . William sat up and rubbed his eyes because it was a surreal situation; his grandfather had been dead for years. Walter was holding a present with a card saying, "Happy birthday from your friend Aesacus." William ripped the paper off the present, and as he did so he felt a strange tightening around his heart. It occurred to him that the feeling might be the slight hint of emotion. Then he rejects the possibility because it is clearly ridiculous. In the box, there was a miniature ship, a small doll's cradle and a toy video camera. Getting up from the rocking chair, his grandfather exclaimed, "That tight feeling around the heart is called happiness. Wonderful, isn't it? One day, just like your parents, you will learn to move someone's heart with your words; you'll be able to evoke sublime thoughts to melt the iciest heart."

A ringing sound filled the air, drowning out Walter's last words. William woke up and sat up in bed. It was still dark outside. No spirit had paid him a visit from the afterlife, his grandfather had been dead for years, it had all been a strange dream. He was in his bedroom and someone had just rung the doorbell. His alarm clock said 3:47 a.m., who could it be at that hour? Taking his pistol, he rushed to the front door and opened it quickly, but no one was there. Just as William, perplexed, was about to close the door, he noticed something on the ground, an envelope. He picked it up and carried it inside. There was a piece of paper inside the envelope with a message written in red ink with a fountain pen. The handwriting was as elegant as the work of a calligraphy artist. The message read: "You will find the answers to your questions at Minedal-e Corporation at Disgust City 45. They have been watching you for some time. Trust no one."

Someone seemed to be guiding him in his investigation, though William couldn't see why. He went to his room in an attempt to get some more sleep, putting the pistol carefully under his pillow just in case, but his mind was so full there was no way he could even close his eyes.

Early the next morning he went to the police station, arriving well before his shift so as not to give John the impression that he was unreliable. The two of them spent the whole day trawling the city, but nothing in particular happened. It was true that police life wasn't very action-packed. In a way, William had been lucky to arrest a dealer at the stadium, John said it had been the only exciting event of his career.

It was now time to return to the station, but John decided to stop and buy something to drink on the way, so he pulled over and told William to wait in the car, he wouldn't be long. He crossed the street to a vending machine, but after about five minutes John was still fiddling with the contraption that had likely swallowed his money without dispensing a drink. William decided to join his colleague and lend him a hand. He got out of the car but had only gone a few feet when he was suddenly blinded by an intense light, a car with headlights full on was bearing down on him at high speed, obviously intending to run him over. He threw himself in John's direction and was nearly crushed. As he fell, he hit his head and knee hard on the pavement. John ran to him. "Are you all right?"

His boss's voice seemed muffled, as if he had a gag covering his mouth. "Open your eyes. Can you hear me?"

With his hand William touched his forehead, trying to ascertain the damage. His head hurt and suddenly everything went black, as if someone had turned out the light.

When he awoke, he was in a hospital ward with an IV attached to his arm and a thumping headache. John was sitting opposite him, absorbed in a magazine, but after a few minutes, realizing that he was awake, he said, "I've never seen so much happen in such a short time. How do you feel, Will?"

"A bit dazed, but I think I'm all right. What did the doctors say?"

"You'll be OK. You sustained a head trauma and minor damage to your knee. I've already sent an incident report to the station. The car that almost did you in is a red Whilson without plates. Can you remember anything else?"

"Not much, to tell the truth."

"OK, if anything comes to mind you can always add it to the report as soon as you get back to work. It seems to have been an accident, maybe the driver was crazy. The doctors have ordered you two weeks' rest."

John rose and went to the door. As he was leaving, he turned and said, "Before I forget, McMillan sent me to check out an old, abandoned building at Calicraston Ville that you had mentioned to him. It wasn't hard to find because it was the only one in the area. It's under sequester, but we got permission to enter anyway, and except from a hell of a lot of dust, there was nothing odd inside. Now get some rest because you need it."

William just nodded his head as a goodbye. He was sure that he had seen the skeletons inside that building, and he was just as sure that it was the resistance headquarters. At that moment a nurse came in wearing a white top with her dark hair tied back. She said her name was Hygieia and after asking about his condition, she began to busy herself with the IV tubes. At one point the cuff of her right forearm rose slightly, revealing a tattoo of a bowl with a snake coiled around it, beneath which were the two stylized letters: "M" and "C."

"It could have been the acronym for Minedal-e Corporation!" he thought. He decided to ask the nurse what the tattooed initials stood for. She didn't seem surprised by the question and replied calmly that they were the initials of her husband, Milton Capersson. He nodded. He had studied enough psychology at the academy to recognize the symptoms of paranoia. It struck him that his fear was beginning to get out of hand. It wasn't normal to be so suspicious and see enemies absolutely everywhere. Maybe no one had tried to kill him after all and it was only an accident, just like it was only a coincidence that someone had broken into his apartment.

3.1

After a few days, he checked himself out of the hospital. He still felt weak and decided to stay home and rest. But the following week he felt well enough to go shopping, then made up his mind to take the car and pay a visit to Minedale Corporation where maybe he would find some answers to his questions and could finally put his mind at ease. He held to the hope that there was no conspiracy awaiting him set up by an elusive secret organization.

He stopped the car in front of the video intercom at the entrance to the pharmaceutical company where a private security guard came up to ask if he had an appointment. William answered that he did not and held up his police badge specifying that he was not there in an official capacity but that he wanted to see Dr. Shelton Malthen. The guard disappeared into his glass booth and communicated with a colleague by two-way radio. A few minutes later he reappeared to say that William had permission to go in despite not having an appointment. Dr. Shelton Malthen would see him.

He left his car in the parking lot at the front entrance of the pharmaceutical company's main building. The branch of Minedal-e Corporation was made up of several dark red buildings scattered over a wide expanse of land filled with trees and well-tended lawns; it seemed more of a luxury resort than a pharmaceutical company.

He entered the main building and walked up to reception. Behind a desk sat a secretary dressed in a dark blue uniform with an earpiece at one ear. On the wall behind her was the company logo: a large triangle within a circle containing crossed swords and the initials "M" and "C." The secretary politely handed him a cup of water and said to make himself comfortable on the couch because the president would soon be free to see him. He took a sip of the water, but it had a bitter taste, maybe from the plastic cup having been too long in its packaging.

After about ten minutes, the secretary rose and asked him to follow her down a corridor of large colored glass windows framed in lead rather like the stained glass you'd find in an old church. At the end of the corridor was a double door of inlaid wood that the secretary opened, inviting him to go in. Behind an enormous desk, the president was expecting him. He had a trim, proud appearance, his thick gray hair was neatly-combed, and his large green eyes and vigorous eyebrows stood out from his face. He was wearing a blue suit with a white shirt while his tie was pink and matched the pocket square in his top pocket. Apart from the olive and rosewood desk, the room had very little furniture, with the exception of a large bookshelf with about a thousand books lined up on its shelves.

"Good morning, I'm William Pattern. Thank you for seeing me, Dr. Shelton Malthen."

"Please call me David. We don't much like formalities here because we'd rather focus on the substance of things. Are you here to make a police inquiry?"

"Well, no, this is actually an informal visit, and you are not obliged to answer my questions."

"Why would I be so rude? Go ahead, tell me, what brings you here today?"

"So not far from Calicraston Ville, there's an abandoned building that was once a recording studio, the building is under sequester and seems…"

Dr. Shelton Malthen interrupted him, "Yes, I know the place and can satisfy your curiosity. A long time ago my father saved the world. He was a great scientist, and we are all here today thanks to his invaluable work. After sleepless nights working on the lethal Coris-91 virus, he discovered a way to defeat it and developed a vaccine. However, members of a terrorist organization called Emosemvi, believing that the vaccine would kill millions of people rather than save them, carried out a series of attacks on our laboratories. They were, of course, wrong, and history has proved them such because the population of the world was saved. And yet these unscrupulous terrorists set up a proper resistance organization with affiliates spread over the world.

Their headquarters were at Calicraston Ville and from there they ran many illegal operations."

"So those of Emosemvi were criminals…"

"Of course! This criminal scum is responsible for the deaths of millions. The disconcerting thing is that the organization had a large following and day-by-day seemed to acquire more converts, so the government started to hunt them down. My father Paul did not agree with such harsh action being taken against them, after all he was a peace-loving scientist. Still, once we started to be attacked, we hired private security guards. One day the police raided the building at Calicraston Ville, bringing the criminal resistance organization to an end. Fortunately, today Emosemvi is only a memory, but it is a stain on the history of humanity, which is why it is not even mentioned in the history books."

"Ah, now it is all clear. Thank you for telling me what really happened. I've one last question for you. Were the members of the terrorist organization able to experience emotions?"

"Don't be silly, of course not! It is still not clear what was motivating their actions. It was most likely a phenomenon of mass suggestion. The leaders of Emosemvi disappeared into thin air or perhaps they all committed suicide. And to keep my father's memory alive, statues of him were put up in the city squares all over the country. I'm sure you have seen them."

David pointed his index finger to a large painting hanging on the wall, a portrait of his father.

William glanced at it for a second. He had the feeling that he had seen Paul Shelton Malthen before, but he couldn't remember where; his face was vaguely familiar. Then he said, "I think I've seen your father before."

"Of course, you would know his face, as I told you, a great many statues were erected in his honor."

"OK, thank you for your time, and for seeing me without an appointment. You are heir to a great tradition, and it was an honor to meet you."

"The pleasure was mine. I wish you all the best for your career in the police."

Once he had left the building, William got into the car and headed for home, thinking about what he knew as he drove. If the resistance had been destroyed, who had left the envelope with the message on the landing outside the door to his apartment?

His patrol chief John Apate had said that he had found no skeletons in the building at Calicraston Ville. Who had removed them? But for the moment he didn't have enough elements to provide answers to those questions. He would have to look harder to find the truth.

4. Surprise in the eyes

William got home and was about to take a shower when someone knocked on the door. With his gun in the holster, he went to answer it. His neighbor Beatrice had come to invite him to dinner at her place. He accepted eagerly, but he would have liked more time to get ready. Even though he didn't know her well, he felt powerfully drawn to Beatrice and hoped she might feel the same. He jumped into the shower, threw on some clothes, dug a container of Mississippi Mud ice cream out of the freezer so as not to come empty-handed and knocked on his neighbor's door. Beatrice was wearing an ankle-length dress, her hair tied up. He gazed at her, dazzled by her beauty, and found himself speechless. After a silence, Beatrice exclaimed, "Should I set the table on the landing or are you going to come in?

"Yeah, I mean... you look great in that dress."

"Thanks. I like sincere people."

She spoke with disarming irony, something that appealed to William, and a second before crossing the threshold he felt a strange sensation in his chest, a tightening around his heart, and then had another sudden hallucination. He saw Beatrice dressed as a bride, in a long ivory gown, with a gold wedding band on her finger. The vision was gone in a flash. Then Beatrice took William's hand and gently drew him into her apartment. Like waking from a dream, he rubbed his eyes. He didn't know why he was having these hallucinations, it definitely was not normal.

Beatrice's place was large, bright and decorated in country style. They walked into the living room where the table was set for two. Placed on a pink tablecloth, the wine glasses and cutlery sparkled, all very elegant. William realized he was still carrying the ice cream and handed it to Beatrice who thanked him and offered him a glass of wine. He put a hand up politely to refuse the wine away because he didn't like to drink on an empty stomach, but Beatrice was adamant, saying, "We have to toast, and wine is the best thing for that."

"I know, but I'd rather drink a bit later."

"It's not like you have to drive home or anything. Don't offend me."

For a second, he was lost in her deep blue eyes. Then, he took the glass and drank the wine.

If they had been born into a different world, one in which emotions could shine their warmth into the hearts of others, this dinner would have likely ended in a passionate kiss. In the space of an instant, this would have sealed their promises of love; then laughing happily they would have whispered sweet nothings and their heartbeats would have come into synch with the notes of destiny. But nothing of the sort happened. At the end of the dinner, they just shook hands and said a formal goodbye. William returned to his apartment and went to bed. But that night he had no dreams.

The next day he woke early and read a book of poetry, as many people did though without really understanding the meaning. Then he picked up a psychology book and spent the rest of the day thinking about last night's hallucination.

It wasn't the first time that it had happened, and the strange sensation in his chest struck him as abnormal. He thought he must have some sort of problem with his heart, he would definitely need to see a neurologist and cardiologist.

By now the evening had begun to cast its shadows through the large windows of the apartment, so he decided to have another look at the wedding video in which his mother appeared. As the images went by, he noticed something odd. Among the people present in the film there was one with a face familiar to him, it was an elegant man in a top hat. More from conditioned reflex than because he really felt the emotion of surprise, he opened his eyes wider. He couldn't believe it: it was Paul Shelton Malthen, the scientist who had found and developed the vaccine and the savior of humanity whose portrait hung in his son's office at the pharmaceutical company's headquarters. What was he doing there? Did Madeline know him? William was contemplating this conundrum when there was a knock at the door. He went to open it but once again there was no one there, only an envelope with the Emosemvi logo lying on the floor. He tore down the stairs because whoever had left it couldn't have gotten far.

He ran out into the street, but as often in that season, it was raining and the sidewalk was thick with people beneath umbrellas, so it was impossible to identify the mysterious messenger. Back in the apartment, he opened the envelope. Inside was a card with a message written in the same fountain pen and red ink, "See you tomorrow at 7 a.m. at Contempt City Cemetery, Zone 4, Section C."

Someone from Emosemvi wanted to get in touch with William, but he trusted no one. He had, in fact, decided to arrest anyone he found who was part of the terrorist organization.

The following day he drove to the cemetery, which was out in the countryside beyond Contempt City. He decided to leave his car at the edge of the street about half a mile from the cemetery because he feared for his safety and wanted to ensure an escape route in case of danger. Climbing plants were everywhere and nearly covered the great entrance gate that was gradually being consumed by rust. A part of the brick enclosure had collapsed, invading a small patch of grass with its rubble. There were no flowers lying at the foot of the gravestones in the cemetery; in truth, rituals for the dead were a relic of the past, now in ruins. No one was moved to go to the grave of their departed loved ones and remember them, such a thing no longer made way it into the hearts of the people. What's more, Contempt City did not now have a maintenance staff for the cemetery. It was falling apart and seemed all the gloomier. If someone killed William there, no one would ever find his body. It was the perfect spot for murder and also, obviously, to get rid of the evidence, so he pulled out his pistol.

After he came into the cemetery, he headed straight to Section C, an area scattered with small chapels and, judging by the coats of arms engraved on them, the occupants had belonged to noble families.

The forlorn spot didn't make William uncomfortable because he liked the feeling of being surrounded by the history of the world and not far beneath him by the remains of people who were practically more alive to emotion than those still on earth.

Beside the metal door to one of the chapels, there suddenly appeared a strange man wearing a black raincoat, sunglasses and a wide-brimmed hat. With a movement of his hand the man beckoned to him. It was impossible to see who he was, but his voice sounded somewhat familiar. "Were you followed?"

"Stuart! Is that you?"

It was Officer Stuart, the man who showed him around the police station on his first day. William would never have expected to find him there.

"Yes, it's me. Listen carefully because there isn't much time!" he exclaimed forcefully.

"Are you here in an official capacity? Is this a police operation?"

Without saying a word, Stuart rolled up his sleeve to reveal his forearm and on it the tattoo of a white mask with three red tears just below the holes for the eyes. William wavered for a moment, he couldn't believe his eyes. Stuart was a member of the resistance! According to Shelton Malthen, it was a criminal organization, on an impulse he pointed his pistol at him, intimating that he should give himself up. Stuart took a step back, sighed deeply as if he were about to make a confession in front of a judge and said, "You don't know what's going on, do you? The resistance took a major blow, but it hasn't been completely wiped out. I can experience emotions and it's fantastic. I feel so alive! What you've heard isn't really what happened, there is another version of the story. Please put the gun down and give yourself the chance to see the world in color because now you are living in a sad, faded reality."

"OK, but you've got two minutes to convince me, then I am going to arrest you and take you back to the police station!"

"Listen to me William. Emotions have always existed, but one day at Minedal-e Corporation they decided to eliminate them because they made people weak and inspired them to do heinous and cruel things. The world was on the verge of extinction, wars abounded, and murder was increasing exponentially. On social networks people rarely exchanged affectionate words. They were always arguing, virtual spaces had become full of hate, worse than a circle of hell. In agreement with a few politicians, Paul Shelton Malthen developed a serum called Em 0 that could inhibit and gradually erase emotions in human beings. Obviously, there were also financial objectives behind all this."

"I can't believe it Stuart!"

"You should! The serum was mixed with the vaccine that countered the terrible virus that was decimating the world population and so began mass vaccinations. By the way, somehow the serum is also able to erase some memories. To this day, all infants get an injection at birth that contains the serum to inhibit emotions. As a result, their whole lives they are deprived of joy, anger and even sadness. They are made into empty boxes!"

William felt confused. He was finding it hard to believe his colleague's absurd story and he didn't understand how a police officer could belong to an illegal organization such as the resistance.

Stuart went on, speeding up his account because he was feeling nervous and wanted to leave the gloomy graveyard as soon as possible, "You must realize that every emotion is useful, there are no negative emotions, even sadness has a specific function. But, for some reason, there are certain people, like you and your father, on whom the serum Em 0 doesn't have the full effect."

"Are we resistant to it in some way?"

"Yes! David Shelton Malthen decided to continue his father's work, seeking out such cases and inoculating them with EM 0 a second time without them knowing. Let me explain. People who were resistant to Em 0 occasionally experienced emotions and this encouraged them to carry out certain actions. If for example someone felt happiness, in all probability it would drive them to experience more, by composing love poetry for instance. Administering a second dose of Em 0, Shelton Malthen erases the memories tied to these very actions, so that no trace of the poetry will remain in their mind."

"Stuart, what if people who are resistant to it keep on feeling emotions after more Em 0 is given them?"

"The people on whom the serum does not have the full effect and on whom the active ingredient no longer manages to contain the emotions, are killed by men from Minedal-e or by government agents. They are everywhere and work undercover, so we can trust no one! They appear to be administering the serum to you in some way. I don't know how but they are. If you have ever had a vivid hallucination you know what I'm talking about... they were not hallucinations; they're the real memories of your life!"

William couldn't believe what he was hearing. "So I don't have hallucinations, they're memories, like the one of Beatrice with the ivory wedding dress and the wedding ring," he thought, bringing a hand to his forehead. Then, seized by curiosity, he looked at Stuart straight in his eyes and asked: "You mentioned my father but he died in a car accident before I was born. What do you know about my parents?"

The rumble of a car engine echoed among the graves. Quickly, Stuart turned to look towards the rusty entrance gate, he exclaimed, "There's no time left, they're here. Tun for it. I'll get back in touch with you!"

Stuart pressed a matchbox into William's palm and rushed off. William ran to the entrance of the cemetery where two men in black were standing guard. So he changed tack and hurried to where the perimeter wall had collapsed leaving a gap, then he hid behind a gravestone, but he was spotted by one of the men who opened fire on him without thinking twice, the bullets whistled over his head and lodged in the wall.

When he realized that the man in black had emptied his magazine and stopped to replace it, he took advantage of the moment to run to the gap in the wall and throw himself through it. Then he got to his feet and ran in the direction of the car, hoping to find it where he had left it and gave a sigh of relief when he saw it. He jumped in, turned on the ignition and shot off with tire rubber burning. As he drove home, he felt disoriented and couldn't stop thinking about Stuart's words. On the one hand, David, son of an eminent scientist, condemned the resistance organization and its acts of terrorism, on the other a police officer gave a very different version of the facts. For now, he couldn't draw any conclusions, but he had to get to the bottom of it all to discover the truth.

William went home. The next day he would go and talk with Chief McMillan, a person he could certainly trust.

The matchbox Stuart had thrust into his hand appeared not to bear any kind of secret message. There was only an advertisement for an old movie theater called "Eversten 66."

4.1

That night William couldn't sleep a wink. Early the following morning he went straight to the police station, he thought he might meet Stuart in the entrance hall and hoped to pump him for more information on his parents. He wouldn't go until Stuart had spit it out! But when he got to the police station there was a different officer on duty. William asked him if he knew a colleague by the name of Stuart, but he said he'd never heard the name before.

At that point, he headed for McMillan's office and knocked, but there was no reply. Presumably, the chief was somewhere in the building. He walked over to the elevator meaning to go back down to the first floor, but no sooner had the elevator doors opened than McMillan stepped out. He said good morning hurriedly and went towards his office. William ran after him, saying, "Good morning, sir. May I speak to you for a moment?"

"Pattern, shouldn't you be at home convalescing?"

"Yes, I should, but I've got something important to tell you."

"I'm in a bit of a hurry today. Could you come back tomorrow?"

A man in a red jumpsuit with an untamed beard and long white hair was polishing the floor with a rag near the elevator door and seemed to be listening to the conversation between William and McMillan. In the top right pocket of his jumpsuit was a badge saying "Tim" and that he was the police station janitor. He looked shabby and didn't inspire much confidence. A frown crossed the face of the janitor for a fraction of a second as if he were able to feel the emotion of anger. William noticed the expression appear briefly on Tim's face, but he was too busy just then to attribute importance to the fact. He turned back to Richard McMillan and lowered his voice, "It will only take a minute, sir. Can we go into your office?"

The chief of police rolled his eyes upwards and walked on towards his office. Once he had closed the door with a bang, he asked, "So what is it that is so urgent?"

"I must talk with you about something very important. I have been approached by a member of the resistance. He started blathering about Minedal-e Corporation plotting against humanity…"

McMillan interrupted him brusquely, "Yes, yes, I know. It's an old story. There is no resistance, only the odd lunatic who amuses himself waging war against capitalism and the big industrial companies. Now go home and take it easy."

"Sir, Stuart isn't down in the hall. Do you know where he's gone?"

"We have hundreds of officers with that name. I don't know every single one of them."

"I mean the colleague who brought me to meet you when I first got here from the academy. Do you remember?"

"Yes, I remember vaguely, maybe he's been transferred to another police station."

"Sir, he's the terrorist! He told me a whole bunch of lies. He was talking about a plot and a sort of serum that could inhibit emotions!"

"I'll tell you what, William. I can't remember exactly who this Stuart is, but if you are right and he is a terrorist, I promise to circulate his photo to all the police stations and have him arrested. The world is now at peace. There are no more wars and criminals have almost disappeared from the face of the earth. They say that when the human species felt emotions it was brought to the verge of extinction. Unfortunately, there are still those who like to invent stories about plots and betrayal."

McMillan went to his desk and opening a drawer pulled out a small bottle of rum, filling a glass he handed it to William and invited him to drink. He didn't much want a drink and he wasn't there to celebrate. Really, he thought McMillan's gesture completely out of place. How could he be thinking of drinking at a time like this?

Noticing William's reluctance to accept the rum, the chief of police encouraged him, "Come on, don't be shy!

Knock it back and you'll find it'll all become clearer. Then go home and rest, that's what you need. I will look into this and if I find Officer Stuart, I will interrogate him and get at the truth."

He drank a mouthful of the rum and thanked the chief, in the end, though he could be a bit thorny, he was reasonable. He felt he had done his duty and been loyal to the police force.

McMillan accompanied him to the door making a gesture for him to leave, then he added, "You just need some rest. Don't believe those legends, because everything is under control. All the stories about a plot, serum and abandoned cemeteries will pop like a soap bubble now. Look after yourself."

The chief closed the door, but outside William suddenly froze. He had never mentioned to McMillan that he had met Stuart at the cemetery. How could he have known about that? It could have been a coincidence or more likely the police were already investigating the case and McMillan did not want to reveal anything yet.

5. The face of emotions

Once he got home, William looked on the internet to find the location of the "Eversten 66" movie theater as it was written on the matchbox Stuart had handed him at the Contempt City cemetery. The only movie theater with a similar name was at Anger City and it was called "Eversten" and not "Eversten 66." As night fell, he set off in the car for Anger City, a poorer and less well-kempt city than the others nearby. The public buildings had not been renovated for some time, though a development plan for urban improvement was about to be set in motion to give it a facelift.

The Eversten now stood abandoned, like all the places where people would meet to have fun in the past. Once, being an actor was quite a well-paid job, but now it was no longer even considered a profession. Of course, if an actor can't simulate a certain state of mind or express emotions by minimal facial mimicry, the public would find it hard to appreciate his performance.

The doors into the movie theater were held shut with heavy wooden planks, while the glassed booth where they used to sell tickets was covered in dust. Skirting the building, William entered a narrow alleyway at the side where there was a rusty fire escape hanging high above his head. He pushed a large garbage can under it and managed to reach it and climb up. He made it to the roof of the movie theater where there was a skylight ajar and, attached to the handle, there was a long rope that reached to the floor inside the room below. Someone had obviously used the rope to go in and out of the movie theater. William hoped that he wouldn't find a nasty surprise waiting inside.

He began to lower himself into the movie theater, but the rope was too worn and couldn't hold his weight. It soon broke and he fell into space. Cushioned armchairs softened his fall and sent a huge cloud of dust up to the ceiling. All the doors were locked and there seemed to be no way out of the room. At the center, there was an old projector with a wire hanging off it that William pushed into an electric socket. A screen with a keyboard lit up. It seems you needed a password in order to work the projector, and William had no clue what it might be. He tried typing in the name of the resistance organization "Emosemvi," but a red X appeared on the screen, and he realized that he had three attempts before the system blocked any chance of turning on the projector. He typed in "Minedal-e," but again nothing happened, except another red X appeared on the screen to indicate that the second attempt had failed. He had one more chance and tried to concentrate so as not to make another mistake. Suddenly, he remembered the message in the envelope left on the landing outside his apartment, "You will find the answers to your questions at Minedal-e Corporation at Disgust City 45. They have been watching you for some time. Trust no one."

At first, when he had read the message he hadn't noticed, but thinking about it now, the number 45 had no connection to the name of the city, so he typed it on the keyboard.

On the matchbox Stuart had given him at the cemetery, the movie theater advertisement read "Eversten 66." Here again, the number 66 seemed irrelevant to the name of the movie theater. So he typed in the number 66, creating the numerical series: "4566." In the deep silence of the hall, the old projector creaked to life, projecting on a large screen the image of a man; he had chestnut hair that was beginning to turn white, regular features fitting in with the symmetry of his face, and in his dark eyes you could make out the spark of a lively intellect. The man was being filmed at the abandoned recording studio in Calicraston Ville. He had on a blue jumpsuit identical to the ones worn by the skeletons that William had found before.

The man said, "If everything has gone wrong, they will already have killed me, and I will not be here waiting for you in person. I can only leave you this video in the hope that it will open your eyes. They have taken over my house, and I'm sure they'll have destroyed all photos of me. You will have no idea who I am, but fate will find a way. William, I am your father Virgilio and I am a member of the resistance organization called Emosemvi. We each use a false name to avoid revealing our identity, and mine is Mike. We members of the resistance experience emotions. In our lives, singing and listening to music make sense as do laughing and hugging someone to show affection."

At that point, Virgilio's eyes shone, and tears fell from them. At first, William didn't understand what was happening, but then he realized how emotions could trigger physiological reactions like crying. If he had been able to cry, too, he certainly would have.

The skeleton in the blue jumpsuit that he had found at the old recording studios, which had a letter from Jacqueline addressed to Mike sticking out of his breast pocket, were the remains of William's father. As fate would have it, he remembered putting a pen decorated with a red plastic rose in the buttonhole of his jumpsuit.

Virgilio continued to speak from the screen, "My son, for some reason there are people, like you and me, on whom Minedal-e Corporation's Em 0 serum does not have the full effect. Somehow, we are more sensitive to external stimuli and, despite the serum's inhibition, can feel a sort of echo of emotion. I was sure that I needed to see a brain specialist because I kept having vivid hallucinations, but then I discovered that these were fragments of memories. The serum deprived me of the best memories of my life, and especially the emotions connected to them. Maybe I am giving you too much information all at once. Let me explain better."

Virgilio drank some water, paused, and with a sad expression but a firm voice continued, "When I was born, they injected me with Em 0, then when I was an adolescent the men from Minedal-e realized, maybe because I sometimes showed emotions through facial expression, that the serum hadn't work on me 100%. So, without my knowing it, they administered further doses of Em 0. I don't know how they did it, because I never got a shot other than the one on the day of my birth. In any case, the government of this country and Minedal-e wanted to control the world, and they succeeded in their objective. Think about it, a world without emotions is more easily manipulated. People deprived of emotions and without a soul never rebel. If there are no demonstrations in the streets, the police are no longer needed. And politicians' speeches don't arouse any emotion and so have no effect on the people, who can't think critically anymore. Now money is only used to buy basic necessities, and few people spend it on recreation. Guess who holds 80% of the shares in the factories that make basic necessities? Minedal-e, and the remaining 20% is in the hands of the government. With no one capable of opposing unjust laws, they can make a lot of money, and that's the aim of that pharmaceutical company."

William could hardly believe what he saw; he was even holding his breath in order not to miss a word said by his father, who was looking around him warily as though he feared he might be in danger.

"Unfortunately, I don't have much time because the men from Minedal-e have discovered where we're hiding, and we must destroy the promotional material. But there is a cure. We know how to cancel out the effect of Em 0. You have to go to Sadness City. In the main square is a café called the Somtlose, and the owner is a woman named Rosie. If she has been identified as a member of the resistance and assassinated, you can talk to her children, and they'll tell you what to do. In the resistance, we use a code to signal that we are part of the resistance and not a government spy. As we talk, we include words that refer to emotions while showing micro-expressions on our faces. Jacqueline, our psychologist, will quickly explain how it works."

The video camera focused on a blond woman, wearing a blue jumpsuit and large round glasses. In a bright voice she said, "OK, so… I would have liked to meet you, but if you're watching this video it means they've killed me. I regret nothing in my life, and I am happy because at least I will have gone to my grave taking my memories and emotions with me."

After a pause, Jacqueline had trouble going on because she was overcome with sadness. Virgilio laid a comforting hand on her shoulder to encourage her to go on. She pulled herself together and continued, "We don't have time for a full lesson, and you won't find what I'm going to tell you in books because censorship by the government and Minedale has hit all the media outlets. The human face has 43 muscles that can produce a range of about 10,000 different expressions. When an emotion is aroused, on a neural level, a process is activated that is translated into a mimic expression. By nature, facial micro-expressions never occur by chance. They always express emotions. The muscles of the face are directly linked to the areas of the brain that become active as soon as an emotion is experienced. While most facial expressions last longer than a second, micro-expressions only last from a fifth to a twenty-fifth of a second. Such brevity prevents an inexpert eye from detecting them, and it takes extensive training to do it."

The woman paused again briefly to rearrange her thoughts and wipe away her tears. Though she tried to be brave, the very idea of risking her life made her quiver. In a trembling voice, she went on, "It'll be easy to tell who is in the resistance because as they speak, they will use our code. They will use the common expressions that refer to an emotional state, like, "I am happy," or "I hate that person," or "That movie makes me sad." As they say these phrases, they will produce facial micro-expressions. If you notice such things it means that you can trust them. The government agents and people from Minedal-e do not feel emotions and are not able to spot facial micro-expressions. Only we, members of the resistance, have broken the chains so as not to be assimilated into an unjust system. I think your father wants to add something more."

Virgilio turned the video camera back until once again it was focusing on his face, "In your grandfather's library, next to a book of poems that I wrote a long time ago, there is a large tome called *The Cosmos and its Mysteries.* Don't mind the title because it's only an old psychology book, but inside is the explanation of how emotions work as well as facial micro-expressions and body language. Study it well and practice in front of a mirror until you can replicate the various facial expressions perfectly. One more thing, my boy. The time has come to talk about your mother. It gives me great pain to say this, but..."

A sudden loud noise caught Virgilio's attention, hurriedly he said, "That was a gunshot! They're coming!"

The recording stopped, leaving William speechless.

5.1

He was surrounded by the solitude of a dusty old movie theater, and his father had just spoken to him from the grave. He didn't know how long he stood there staring at the blank screen, but when he came back to himself, the sun had already gone down, and the rays of the moon were filtering through the small skylight on the roof down into the room. The moon, moved to compassion for humanity and particularly for the man inside the movie theater, had decided to caress his face with its translucent rays, made hazy by the thick dust in the room.

He had to get out of there but had no idea how. The doors were shut from the outside, and he certainly couldn't open them with his bare hands. He'd need a heavy axe or a crowbar at least. His cell phone was almost dead, but there was enough battery left to make a quick call to his academy friend Leonardo, who picked up right away and was amazed to hear William's story and especially his odd request for help. Leonardo worked for the police in Sadness City and that evening he was on patrol with the car somewhere not far away, so he headed for the movie theater with sirens blaring. In the meantime, William had managed to extract the film from the projector and set fire to it in a metal bucket to avoid it falling into the wrong hands.

Soon afterwards, Leonardo seemed to have arrived because someone was banging on the doors with something heavy. A few minutes later the doors sprang open, and William was able to get out. As soon as Leonardo saw him, he handed him a bottle of water and asked, "Will, what are you doing here at this hour?"

"Listen, something terrible is going on. I can't tell you any more now, but I've got to get to Café Somtlose in Sadness City."

"I'll come with you if you want, but there are better places to have a coffee."

"You don't understand, Leo. The Somtlose is a base of the resistance. The owner is one of them and appears to have critical information to change the world."

"Resistance? That's just an old legend. Will, the world doesn't need to be changed because it's perfect just as it is. There are no more bar brawls, no more war. Friendships don't end because of jealousy, and when someone dies no one suffers. My father always tells the story of a neighbor and his three-year-old son. One day a car accidentally ran over the little boy while he was riding his tricycle in front of the house. If the father had felt emotion, he would have been tortured by pain, but he simply picked up his son and called an ambulance, without batting an eye."

"Leo, you don't get it. We have to go to the Somtlose!"

"OK, let's do this: I'll take you home because you seem in a daze, you take a shower and a rest, then tomorrow I'll pick you up in my car, because I'm on duty now and I can't wander about the place chasing a phantom resistance organization. Don't worry about leaving your car here. Later I'll call a tow truck and have it left outside your house."

William nodded and got in his friend's car, which took him home. As soon as he was over the threshold he sat on the couch and gave a heavy sigh. He thought about his father's remains at the abandoned recording studios. Who knows where they took them to get rid of them. In his heart he was hoping he would find out where they were so at least he could give him a decent burial. He was thinking about what Virgilio had said, then he sat bolt upright and quickly went over to the bookshelf, hurrying up the bronze library ladder. At first, he couldn't find what he was looking for, but then, right up in the corner of a top shelf, he found a large book with the title: *The Cosmos and its Mysteries.*

He spent all night reading, every so often he would close his eyes from exhaustion but almost immediately he would open them again not only because he was so fascinated by what he read but also because it added to his training in psychology. It was as though each tile of a huge mosaic were gradually falling into place. That night he learned that the seven basic emotions are: anger, fear, happiness, sadness, disgust, surprise and contempt. Then he discovered how the face expresses each of them, including with facial micro-expressions.

He also found out that when a person in the old world got angry the blood flowed quickly to their hands in preparation for a fight, while adrenalin was produced by the body to let it to respond with heightened strength. When a person felt fear the blood tended to flow into their lower limbs to allow them to respond by flight from danger; this brought blood away from the face, which is why you heard the expression "go pale with fear."

It was extraordinary to William to find that these ancestral biological mechanisms had abandoned the human beings of the modern world.

He found it all very interesting and went on to discover that when long ago a person felt happy, certain cerebral receptors inhibited negative feelings so as to allow their energy to be directed towards new positive objectives, while stimulating the parasympathetic system that induced a state of calm and fulfillment. When people were sad, one of the main biological changes was a decrease of energy and a general slowing down of the metabolism. This was because inner resources were being made available for a future reaction towards what had caused the sadness, such as bereavement or any other unpleasant event. When a person felt disgust, their upper lip moved upwards and their nose wrinkled, which was dictated by the primordial imperative to contract their nostrils so as not to inhale noxious gas in the air and moved their mouth like expelling inedible food that was potentially dangerous to their health. As for surprise, the eyebrows are pushed upwards so as to let more light reach the retina and increase the field of vision in order to react rapidly to an unexpected event. Finally, contempt was shown in the lower part of the face, where the corners of the mouth moved to provoke a rising of the cheeks. Sometimes contempt, usually felt towards people or their actions, was shown by the raising of a single eyebrow.

That night a window opened on a new world in William's mind and he succeeded in reading the entire book and completing the part about facial mimicry, body language, micro-expressions and verbal communication. And he found time to practice simulating the various facial expressions in the mirror.

"Were human mechanisms really so complex? By losing its heritage of emotions it was as though the world had lost its brightest colors, like a painting without a soul. How could two young hearts stop for an instant just as they melted into a tender embrace? How could you do a good deed, helping someone in difficulty, if you couldn't even feel at least a little compassion?" William was mulling over these questions when he was overcome by sleep and slowly closed his eyes.

6. An explosion of emotions

William was still asleep on the couch when Leonardo knocked on the door with some hot coffee and toast. Thanking him, he took a quick shower and joined him in the car. Leonardo was the only person he could really trust. He had always been a loyal friend since their days in the academy.

William was the first to speak, "Thanks, Leo, I appreciate what you are doing for me."

"Friends help each other when they are in trouble. What do you expect to find at the Somtlose?"

"Answers. Then I'll get the chance to contact members of the resistance. I've actually got a colleague at the station who is in Emosemvi."

"Do I know him? What's his name?"

"I don't think so. His name's Stuart. Another time I'll tell you what I've found out."

"We've got plenty of time now, Will. Go ahead."

"No, right now I have to focus on what will happen at the café. It could go smoothly, or someone could try to kill me. When we get there I'll go inside, and you stay in the car with your pistol at the ready, OK?"

"OK."

After driving for miles, they finally got to the main square in Sadness City and parked opposite the café. The place had large glass windows to let the sunlight in, there was a wooden door of an unusual circular shape, and just under the image of a white prancing pony was the wood-burned name, *Somtlose*.

William got out of the car, crossed the street and went into the café, which had a strong smell of coffee and cigars. Addiction to tobacco was a thing of the past, which is why it was so strange to smell cigar smoke in there. The café was decorated in the style of a mountain lodge. There were several wooden tables, small couches covered in green leather and large posters of wild animals on the walls. An elderly woman was sitting at a table sipping from a cup, her white hair carefully tied up beneath a large mother-of-pearl barrette. At her feet lay a mutt, its leash tied to a chair leg, against which a crutch was leaning. Not far from her two men were talking at another table, one of them was wearing a dark blue mechanics' jumpsuit, while the other was dressed in an elegant, checked suit with a brown tie. It seemed a bit off that someone so well dressed should be sharing a table with a mechanic; maybe they were hit men preparing for action? Behind the bar, intent on washing glasses, was a young woman with hair dyed green, and on the back of her hand was a tattoo of a snake with red eyes. Looking closely, even the woman's eyes had a strange reddish tinge.

"Can I have a coffee please?" asked William.

"Sure. My name is Lucy. Anything else you'd like after the coffee, just ask."

"OK, thanks."

As Lucy made the coffee, William was on the lookout for micro-expressions on the woman's face, but he couldn't spot any because Lucy's face was expressionless, exactly like every other human being around. The well-dressed man sitting at the table with the mechanic put a hand in his pocket. Under his coat, William's pistol was in its holster, and he was ready to whip it out. The man pulled out his wallet and, laying it on the table, continued to talk with his friend, at which point William gave a sigh of relief.

Lucy put the coffee on the bar, asking, "Do you want sugar?"

"Yes, thanks. Sugar puts me in a good mood."

"Sorry, what do you mean?"

"Sugar contains substances that make me happy."

On William's face a line went from his nose down to each side of his mouth, the cheeks rose, while small wrinkles appeared at the outer edge of his eyes, what they call "crow's feet." It was, of course, the typical expression of happiness.

"As for me, sugar always makes me think of the past. Children used to love it. If I'm not mistaken, it had a strong sickly-sweet smell," replied Lucy.

As she said these words, she revealed the micro-expression of disgust, raising her upper lip and wrinkling her nose.

William sat on a stool and, putting his elbows on the bar, he looked Lucy straight in the eye and said, "My grandfather often told me fantastic stories about cotton candy, but sadly he died. I miss his stories so much. Nothing can free me of my sadness."

For a fraction of a second, the typical facial micro-expression of sadness appeared on Lucy's face. It only lasted an instant, but it was enough for William to notice the inside ends of her eyebrows rising to meet in the center towards her forehead, while the corners of her mouth turned down.

Now Lucy gestured with her head that he should come back into the kitchen, the door to which was on her side of the bar. William got off the stool and glanced at the old woman and the two men in the café. They all seemed to ignore what was going on beyond their own tables; the old woman was reading a magazine while the two men were talking between themselves. William followed Lucy into the kitchen, and she asked him, "Why are you here?"

"I am William, Virgilio Pattern's son. Is your real name Rosie?"

"Rosie was my mother, but she was killed by the police some time ago. Actually, my real name is Tisiphone, not Lucy. You know that every member of the resistance uses a false name, right?"

"Yes, I know everything."

"Now I'm waiting to be put on trial. The judges have accused me of killing her. They obviously want to frame me. Behind it all is the long arm of that witch from Minedal-e!"

William remembered reading something about a woman at the head of Minedal-e in the letter he found in his father's breast pocket at the recording studios at Calicraston Ville, so he asked, "What is the woman's name? Isn't Shelton Malthen the head of the pharmaceutical company?"

"Some people call her Campe, but no one has ever seen her. The head of the pharmaceutical company isn't Shelton Malthen. He's just a puppet, and someone else is pulling the strings. I don't know any more than that. Now listen, because I have to get back to my customers. I don't know whether you're a free man or not, I mean… I don't know if you can really feel emotions or if before you were just simulating micro-expressions. If so, good work, you're a great actor."

As she was speaking, her facial expressions followed on each other with incredible speed, as if she had let herself go now that she was away from prying eyes. Lucy showed him into the kitchen's cold storage room, and then she moved some wooden boxes that were hiding a trapdoor. The temperature inside the storage room was low. On the ice-covered wall were screws holding a thermostat below which was a strange numeric keypad with twenty keys in the form of golden rings.

Lucy pressed the sequence 3-7-9-1 and the mechanism of the trapdoor sprung open.

"They told me you were coming and I have to give you a message. Please listen carefully," said the woman. "Down here you'll find the serum to reactivate emotions. It's called Reversing. Watch out, because I keep it in a basket with my poisonous snake. In order for the Reversing to have effect, you must inject it with a syringe so that it gets in your bloodstream, and then, within an hour of the injection, you have to experience the seven basic emotions; otherwise it won't work."

"Was the poisonous snake really necessary?"

"He's a very good guardian, but now let me finish explaining. You'll start to notice the first results after a few hours, then gradually the emotions will begin to appear, your facial muscles will slowly wake up, and you will be able to express the emotions. People who inject themselves with Reversing have to remember never to let any emotions show in public, or they they'll end up being identified and killed by the Minedal-e hit men. Those bastards are everywhere! They have spies all over the place and have infiltrated every single public institution. So please, don't tell anyone about our meeting, or it'll be a death sentence for me. Did you come alone or was someone with you?"

"A friend is waiting in the car, but he's trustworthy."

"William, maybe I haven't been clear. Some members of Emosemvi have been betrayed not once but a thousand times, even by their own parents. Do you know how my mother died?"

He shook his head in silence, and she continued her story with growing sadness. "My brother Ronald was at a club in Anger City, and he'd had a bit too much to drink. At one point, as he was talking with a friend, he couldn't help laughing, and suddenly the club went silent, and everybody stared at him. He ran out of the club, but no sooner had he got to his car than two policemen caught him. Once back at the police station he was interrogated for twenty-six hours non-stop until, exhausted, he admitted to being able to feel emotions. So he was handed over to the men from MC."

"They're corrupt!!"

"Unfortunately, that's not all, William. They interrogated him again and promised not to kill him if he gave them the names of resistance members. He didn't give them my name, but he naively only gave that of my mother, thinking that it would save her life. Ronald died that night, and my mother lost her life the next day in an explosion in the kitchen at home. First, the police filed the case away, claiming that it was a mere domestic accident but then they reopened it and accused me of killing my mother."

A tear gleamed at the edge of her eye and slowly made its way down her face.

William felt just like that tear. Most of the time a tear drops straight down the cheek pulled by the force of gravity and ends up on the lips. But sometimes it seems to follow an irregular course, wandering first one way and then sliding down the neck. No one has yet fully understood the laws of physics that govern the movements of tears, which seem to respond to the whims of fate. William, just like that tear, was navigating uncharted waters and did not know where his pursuit, full of twists and turns, would lead him, much less whether his life would end that day or years later.

The woman quickly dried her face and just before leaving the kitchen, she turned and put her finger to her lips to remind William never to reveal their meeting to anyone.

6.1

William opened the trapdoor, and climbing down the steps under it, found himself in a small secret room. Here, inside a basket, next to the snake Tisiphone had told him about was a small bag printed with the white mask and three red tears of Emosemvi's logo. He rolled his coat like a sleeping bag and held it out to the snake to distract it. The snake did its duty right away and sprang into action, biting into the coat, while William managed to quickly grab the little bag. He opened it and found a plastic vial with a label that read: *Reversing*. He put on his coat, put the vial into the pocket and went back up the steps. Then, once he had closed the trapdoor and moved the wooden boxes back over it, he headed for the exit. Lucy was still at the bar. The man dressed as a mechanic and the one with the elegant suit were still talking, but the old woman had gone. William looked out of the café's large windows to the street to check that Leonardo was still in the car. "Great, it's there. It seems that everything went to plan, and I've made it out this time again."

The old woman who had been at the Somtlose could now be seen slowly crossing the street. With her right hand she leaned on her crutch, and in her left she held the dog's leash. Suddenly, she stopped and seemed to turn back to look at the café. Quickly and with no hesitation, the woman put a hand in her pocket and took out an object that appeared to have a red LED light on it, and then she raised the crutch up as though she were waving goodbye to someone in the café and pushed the button on the object in her other hand. William realized too late what was happening and with a leap forward tried to reach the exit. A flash of light shone into the Somtlose, and then, in a fraction of a second there was a loud boom, and the café was suddenly filled with flames. William was thrown out of the entry door and ended up on the sidewalk. His black coat had caught fire, but he managed to take it off and put out the flames. He was covered in dust and surrounded by scattered debris from the force of the explosion. Inside the café, three dead bodies could be glimpsed, one of which was Lucy's. William wasn't able to cry but he felt that strange tightness in his chest provoked by the emotion of sadness, then he decided that it would be right to say goodbye to Lucy using her real name. So staring at the flames, which in the meantime had swallowed up the Somtlose with their inexorable, infernal spirals and were now licking at the sidewalk too, said, "Tisiphone, when I know sadness, I will be able to say goodbye like you deserve."

Meanwhile there was no trace of the old woman. When Leonardo heard the explosion he leapt out of his car and ran over to William. As he helped him up, he asked, "Will, are you all right? What the hell happened?"

"Yeah, I'm OK. Someone was trying to bump me off."

"We need to get you to the hospital for a checkup."

"Listen, Leo, the hospital isn't safe. They'd ask me a lot of questions that I can't answer. Please just take me home."

"Whatever you want. Can you walk?"

"Yeah, I'll manage. Now let's go."

Both of them got into the car and left the place fast, and the sirens of the police and fire department were already echoing in the air as they drove away.

"I'll deal with the police report because I'm in service at Sadness City police station and the Somtlose is in our jurisdiction. What happened back there?" asked Leonardo as he drove.

William rummaged in the pockets of the coat that he was holding and found the vial of Reversing still intact. Fortunately, the explosion seemed not to have damaged it. He trusted Leo and would definitely tell him what had happened, but just then he had an excruciating headache and was feeling rather confused, so he decided to put off all explanations until the next day and only said, "An old woman was sitting at one of the tables in the Somtlose. Then she left and activated a remote-controlled bomb. The place was a branch of the resistance."

"Will, that old story again. When will you stop believing in fairy tales?"

"I'll tell you who I met there, but first I need some rest. Be sure not to tell my boss at the police station what happened today. In your report, just say that you were passing the Somtlose by chance when you heard the explosion. Don't mention my name, OK?"

"All right, no problem."

William closed his tired eyes. When he awoke, he found himself lying on the couch in his apartment, in his hand was a note saying, "Rest up. I'll call you later." Apparently, Leonardo had brought him home, though he couldn't remember for the life of him either getting out of the car or climbing the stairs.

Realizing that he no longer had his coat on, he sprung to his feet, exclaiming, "The vial!"

Wincing from pain, he walked over to the entrance, to find his coat hanging on the back of the front door. He checked the pockets and found the vial. Relieved, he decided to take a shower and rest some more because he was still feeling dazed.

7. As doves...

The next day William woke up late, his head throbbing and with a whistling in his ears. Maybe the explosion had damaged his eardrums or, more likely, caused a temporary side effect. He turned on the television and made some coffee. Just then the news channel was giving the weather forecast, and right afterwards the screen showed a journalist standing outside the Somtlose reporting on the explosion, linked to the newsroom. Behind her you could see the burnt-out café. The journalist commented, "The cause of the incident at the Somtlose in Sadness City is yet to be confirmed. Local people suggest that the long-standing bar, founded thirty-five years ago, was going through a financial crisis. Killed in the explosion were a mechanic and a famous lawyer whose name has not been released yet. Forensic scientists are trying to identify a third body. In all likelihood it belongs to the owner of the café, Lucy Inklings. That is all for now direct from Sadness City. Back to the newsroom."

As he turned off the television the phone rang. Leonardo was calling to check up on him. "Hi, Will, how are you feeling?"

"Better, thanks."

"So have you got your head straight now? What happened at the café yesterday?"

"I can't say much over the phone."

"Don't worry. I'm calling on a secure line."

"I met a member of the resistance. They use a kind of code to work out whether they can trust the person they are talking with. Basically, when two members of the resistance meet, they start to refer to emotions, using phrases like "eating that food makes you happy," or "this music makes you sad." As they say these sorts of things, they show emotions through facial micro-expressions. So if one of the people speaking is not a member of the resistance, they won't notice anything unusual at all, because you need to be trained to notice facial micro-expressions."

"Sounds like science fiction, Will."

"Yet it's true. Remember, don't tell anyone about this."

"Sure, you can count on me."

"I'm not sure, but they may have been expecting me at the café. It's possible that the aim of the bombing wasn't to destroy the resistance café but to do away with me. How did they know that I was going to the Somtlose? Maybe they've got bugs in and are keeping an eye on me."

"Will, I doubt that, but if it makes you feel any better, I can borrow a bug detector from the station, although I don't think there's much point. I can't promise to get it for you right away though. I've got to go now."

"OK, but I haven't told you everything."

"The chief is coming. I'll call you back."

William wanted to tell his friend about Reversing, but there would be time for that.

He went to the medicine cabinet in the bathroom, grabbed a syringe and lay down on the couch. If the serum to restore emotions were actually a poison, it would kill him on the spot. But he decided to risk it, so once he had drawn the serum into the syringe, he injected it into a vein in his left arm. The grandfather clock in the living room was striking 11:30 a.m. Now he had an hour to experience the seven basic emotions, otherwise the serum would not take effect.

He ran to the closet to get another coat. He had several identical ones and needed a replacement for the one from the day before because the fire had ruined it. He didn't need to be dressed, so he stayed in his pajamas, put the coat on, grabbed a hand mirror and left the house to go down to the first floor. Just next to the stairwell there was a way down to the basement. He climbed down the ladder and made his way down the long corridor that led to the boiler room. On the floor there were a row of covers for the sewage system. He lifted one of the covers and took a deep breath, and after coughing in reaction to the nauseating smell, held the hand mirror up to his face and saw that for a moment his top lip was raised, and he had wrinkled his nose. He felt slight pain in his facial muscles as they engaged in the typical expression of disgust. Evidently, the Reversing serum had the effect of holding facial micro-expressions on the face for a few more seconds before disappearing. He quickly closed the cover and went back up to his apartment.

Now he planned to test the emotion of surprise but wasn't sure how to manage it. Other than the general hints given him by Tisiphone, no instruction manual had come with the serum. After thinking a bit about what to do, he left the apartment once again and went down to the street, which at that hour was crowded. He started to push people, trying to get a reaction, but all they did was stare at him until finally someone commented coldly, "You're behaving strangely. Please stop it." At one point, an old woman in a wheelchair, thinking she was being attacked, pulled out pepper spray from her bag. No sooner did William realize this than he opened his eyes wide and his mouth dropped open. Be held up the mirror and noted the look of surprise on his face, but then he quickly closed his eyes tight shut because the woman was spraying the stinging liquid right into his face. The scene was comical, but not so much for William who was rolling on the ground covering his face with his hands. Despite his blurred vision, he managed to rise to his feet and get back home again. Then he ran to the bathroom to wash his face, his eyes were puffy, but he couldn't waste any time because it was running out.

The grandfather clock in the living room struck noon. He opened wide the window and climbed onto the ledge trying to lean against the wall as much as possible so as not to fall off. He certainly didn't want to kill himself, but it was the only way he could think of to experience the emotion of fear. As he stood there, his eyebrows crept close together creating small horizontal wrinkles on his forehead and his lips stretched to the right and left. With little steps he moved back to the window, got back inside and breathed a sigh of relief. His face muscles seemed to have gone numb, maybe because they had never before been used to show emotions.

Time was flying by and he started to think that he might not manage to experience the four last emotions. He turned on the television in the kitchen, tuning in to the news channel where the reporter was again relaying the events at the Somtlose. Based on clues gathered at the site of the explosion, the detectives had managed to reconstruct the entire sequence of events, attributing the cause to the malfunction of a defective propane tank. On hearing the lie, William made the typical expression of contempt, tightening and raising his cheeks and the corners of his mouth, and then he grabbed his coffee mug and threw it towards the television, missing it by a whisker. The contents of the mug ended up all over the wall and the curtain near the window. At the same time he felt anger, his forehead contracted causing his eyebrows to converge downwards, his nostrils to flare, and his lips to clamp tightly together and narrow.

A photo of Tisiphone appeared on the television screen, William felt a tightening in his chest, the internal edges of his eyebrows rose and drew close, while the corners of his mouth bent downwards. He was feeling deep sadness. A tear filled his eye and, incredulous, he touched it with his index finger. When the explosion at the Somtlose happened, he had promised himself that he would give a thought to Tisiphone as soon as he was capable of feeling sadness. So it happened that he dedicated to her the very first tear of his life. He stared at the television for a while, the tumult of emotions making him feel confused and disoriented.

The grandfather clock showed 12:25 p.m. It had been fifty-five minutes since he had injected the serum, and the time left to experience the seven basic emotions was nearly up. If those five minutes went by without him exposing himself to the last emotion, that of happiness, the serum would have no effect and his face would remain expressionless. It was wonderful to feel emotions, and even though he had only just discovered them, William would never give them up now. His head was still full of the images on the television report, so after feeling sadness it seemed practically impossible in such a short time to change his state of mind so completely and experience happiness.

The clock in the living room was about to strike, and as he sat with his head in his hands, an idea suddenly came to him. He leapt up, ran across the landing to Beatrice's place and started knocking insistently on her door. She didn't seem to be home, and his last hopes were waning with each passing second, when Beatrice opened the door. William kissed her passionately, his heart beating wildly, then he pulled back and turned his face away to hide the expression of happiness.

"Are you all right, William?" she said, looking closely at him for a moment, but obviously without showing surprise.

"Yes, I'm fine, sorry. I'm conducting a social experiment."

"A social experiment that involves kissing your neighbor?"

"Yes, exactly."

"So did you also try kissing the old woman in apartment 626?"

To hide his smile, William turned his face away again, then he said, "Well, no, not yet. I mean, it won't be necessary…"

"OK, next time could you give me advanced warning before involving me in your experiments?"

William nodded, and a crazy idea sprang to mind. Maybe Beatrice was in the resistance. He would be able to try to use the micro-expression code with her, and so he said, "I hope I made you happy."

For a fraction of a second, the micro-expression of happiness appeared on William's face.

"What do you mean?" asked Beatrice, impassive.

"Forget it. It's nothing. I've got to go now. I was listening to the news because sad things are happening in the world."

As he spoke, he made the micro-expression of sadness appear on his face.

"What's happening in the world?"

Rather than answer her question, he simply waved his hand in goodbye. For a moment, he had hoped to himself that she might feel emotions too, but he was wrong. As he left, he noticed the necklace around Beatrice's neck from which hung a heart-shaped pendant with the letter "W" engraved in the center.

Back home he noticed the muscles of his face were aching, the serum must have taken effect by now, although he wasn't absolutely certain. He was feeling tired and decided to spend the rest of the day getting his thoughts in order and planning his next move. In the evening, he ate some dinner and went straight to bed because the side effect of the serum was clearly extreme sleepiness.

7.1

When William awoke, the world seemed to have taken on more vivid colors. A ray of sun filtering through the window seemed to glow brighter than the day before, while the faded way things had previously looked, now had a stronger hue. It could be that Reversing also altered the capacity to perceive color in the world. He wondered to himself if the serum had really worked and decided to test it out. He started to think of Beatrice and felt his heart jump, then he thought of David Shelton Malthen and found his fists clenched with anger, and, lastly, he thought of his father Virgilio until the tears poured down his face. Having emotions made him feel alive!

How could human beings live without emotions? He was moved, and his thoughts turned to his mother. Maybe she had been in the resistance, too. Then why was Jacqueline in love with his father? Had Virgilio returned the feeling? For the time being, he didn't know enough to be able to answer such questions.

Still in his pajamas, he went down into the street in order to get a better look at the brightness of things: everything seemed clearer and more vibrant. He gazed in admiration at the bright purple color of a woman's coat as she stood sending a message on her cell phone, then he was struck by the loud colors of a backpack on a passerby, but he became truly awed when his gaze was lost in the vastness of the sky. At that moment he realized exactly how perfect the world had been created, with everything in balance, and yet evil people had managed to deprive humanity of the possibility of perceiving all that beauty. In the old days, people must have taken for granted that they could feel an emotion, without realizing how very precious that ability was.

People were beginning to stare at William, and then some hurriedly looked the other away when it occurred to them that he might be out of his mind. After all, it wasn't entirely normal to be out in the street dressed in pajamas, but what is freedom if not the whisper of a crazy notion?

He got home, dressed and headed to the building's garage. He opened the door and pulled off the sheet covering his motorcycle with its iridescent colors, long left untouched. Here was his true passion, though he didn't even ride it often. The roar of the engine was soon echoing through the garage. William hit the streets of Happiness City, the wind whipping through his hair, and he felt free and, more to the point, full of emotions!

He spent the day on his motorcycle, his eyes often captivated by the landscape around him. He felt like a child discovering the world and even the smallest details touched his heartstrings and made them hum with emotion. He came home late in the evening, and on his way up the stairs he ran into Beatrice. She said hello, and he responded with a smile, and then, realizing his mistake, made his expression neutral. But Beatrice had noticed that smile and started to stare at William, but he looked away and hurried to his apartment. He had to learn to control his emotions and that meant his facial expressions too. He couldn't let himself make mistakes. He went inside and sat on the sofa, not knowing that a video camera had been installed in the eye of a marble statue on the fireplace and was filming him. Someone had broken into his apartment and put it in. Who was spying on him? How long had that camera been there?

The phone rang, and he was surprised to hear Stuart's worried voice saying, "We have to meet. I have something important to tell you. Meet me at the old bowling alley in Happiness City."

"Where have you been, Stuart? No one has seen you at the station."

"We don't have time to talk about it. Do you know the old bowling alley?"

"Yeah, I used to go there with my school friends when I was a kid. I know where it is."

"See you there in an hour."

Stuart abruptly cut off the conversation, hanging up the phone. William wasted no time, grabbed his gun and took off on his bike. On his way to the bowling alley, he tried to think what secrets Stuart might have to tell him. His hand turned lightly on the throttle and the bike picked up speed.

His coat flapped behind him, showing its red satin lining, and, just for that moment, he felt invincible.

Stuart's car was outside the bowling alley. William tried to get in the building from the main door, but it was locked, so he went to the hole in the fence that he used to go through as a kid to sneak inside. He wondered if kids still went to explore that old bowling alley.

As soon as he got inside, he heard a groan from behind a door. He took out his gun and kicked the door down. Stuart was on the ground, pale-faced, and with a gunshot wound.

"What happened?" asked William, putting his hand behind Stuart's head to hold it up.

Stuart coughed twice and answered, "I don't have much time, my friend."

"Tell me who it was!"

"Don't worry about that. What matters is that I tell you what they're planning. All the resistance safe houses are being found. They are destroying us one by one. There must be a spy amongst us. You have to contact another member of the resistance. He works in our station at Happiness City, his name is…"

Stuart had stopped breathing. William tried to resuscitate him but there was nothing he could do. He closed Stuart's eyes with his hand and looked at his face for the last time. As chance or irony would have it, his friend's face looked peaceful, as though he were smiling at death. William knew he couldn't call the police. The news of Stuart's death would probably never be made public.

As he hurtled homeward on his motorcycle, the fiercely powerful wind itself seemed to call a truce with his face from which tears were flowing profusely.

He spent the next few days at home, until his sick leave was up, and the time had come to go back to the office. He got to the police station early in the morning, and in the entrance hall where he had met Stuart the first time there was a different officer on duty. He took the elevator and headed for the office of his boss Richard McMillan, who was on the phone. As he stood there, he had another look at the commemorative award hanging on the wall with the dedication from Minedal-e Corporation. The chief of police couldn't be in cahoots with Shelton Malthen because if he were, he wouldn't keep the commemorative award on the wall of his office, so he must be unaware of it all. While he was absorbed in these thoughts, his colleague John Apate came in. John shook his hand and asked in a vaguely ironic tone, "How was your vacation?"

"Good, I'm better now. Thanks for asking."

The chief of police hung up the phone and started to speak, "Several public places have been blown up recently, and people are disappearing without any apparent reason. We have to find out what's going on. We have gotten an anonymous warning that something strange is happening in a restaurant in Surprise City. Go there and gather as much information as you can."

"Sir, we have no jurisdiction over Surprise City," William pointed out.

"Now we do. I just had a meeting with other chiefs of police, and we've all agreed. As I said, recently, in every city the managers of small businesses have been disappearing. We don't know why, and we have to find out. Now get yourselves over to Surprise City and find out what the hell is going on!"

John and William left the room and took the police car to Surprise City, but on the way something unexpected happened. They had stopped at some traffic lights, when John suddenly said, "Today is a beautiful day. The fresh air cheers me up."

William was so surprised he didn't reply, so John laid it on thick, "Since I started this job fifteen years ago, nothing strange has ever happened to me. The most exciting thing was giving out traffic fines for double parking. Then, you get here, fresh from the academy, and all hell breaks loose. It makes me sad to think of the people who have died and their families."

William stared at him for a while and then, assuming a sad face, said, "Yes, I'm very sorry for them, too."

Obviously, the contact at the police station that Stuart was referring to was his patrol leader.

"Jonathan!" exclaimed John all of a sudden.

"What... sorry?"

"Jonathan is my real name, and I am a free man."

William was struck dumb and couldn't hide his expression of surprise. Breathing deeply and nodding he asked, "OK, what do you know about the resistance?"

"I joined the resistance not long ago. I don't know much but since I injected myself with Reversing my life has changed. The world seems more vivid and full of color. I feel deeply, in a way it's like being born a second time. The resistance doesn't force anyone to use the serum. In fact, you need to earn their trust to get access to it. Have you injected Reversing?"

"Yes, John, and my life has changed for the better. Does the resistance have a plan to stop Shelton Malthen?"

"I don't know. I'm just a newcomer, but rest assured if they want something from you, they'll know how to get in touch. For now, let's keep a low profile because there could be MC spies even at the police station."

John smiled at William, who returned the smile and gave him a pat on the shoulder to reinforce and underscore the understanding between them. Meanwhile they had reached their destination and parked the car outside a restaurant called Marleyes. The main door of the restaurant was bolted shut, and a sign hung on it saying, "Closed for renovation."

A middle-aged man with a long gray beard and paint-splattered clothes came up to them. "I'm George, the owner of Marleyes. Can I help you?"

"We're from the police and may be able to help you. We got a report at the police station and need to ask you some questions. Has anything unusual happened here recently?" asked John.

"Yes... something very unusual. Business has been tough and so instead of calling a construction firm to renovate the restaurant, my son Stan and I decided to do it ourselves. I am really worried about him because last night, while we were finishing painting a wall in the kitchen, two guys turned up at the door, and my son went to talk to them. He didn't come back, and I went to look for him, but when I got to the entrance of the restaurant the door was wide open and he was gone. It's not liked my son to disappear like that. Something must have happened to him. A lot of people have been disappearing lately. It's all you ever hear on TV. Sad things are happening. Maybe the world isn't the safe place people say it is."

"OK, we'll do everything we can to find your son. Don't worry, he'll be OK. We'll expect you at the police station at Happiness City to make your official statement. Bring a picture of the boy along with you, OK?" said John in a reassuring tone.

"Thank you, officer, I appreciate your kindness. I've got a picture here."

George showed them the picture of a man with blond hair, brown eyes and a small scar on his chin. They set a time a few days later for him to go to the police station. Someone from the office would contact him to confirm the exact appointment time.

When George had talked to them, he had mentioned that he was worried about Stan. Then as he went on, he had referred to sadness. In all likelihood, he was a member of the resistance, but William wasn't entirely certain. One thing was for sure though, he had expressed absolutely no emotion on his face.

The two returned to the police station and spent the rest of the day there. William didn't have his own real office, though he had been assigned a cubicle with a desk, computer, telephone and office supplies. It was his workstation, but he hadn't yet used it because until then he had always been on patrol with John.

CHAPTER TWO:

The Bitter Aftertaste of Truth

1. Truth is a hallucination

The days passed quickly, and it was soon Sunday. William would have liked to go for a ride on the motorcycle, but it was pouring rain, so he took the car and headed for downtown Happiness City, taking the elevator to the top floor of the skyscraper where his grandfather Walter used to take him as a boy to admire the view.

Suddenly he had another hallucination, but this time it seemed more vivid than the ones before, much more like a memory. He saw Beatrice at the top of that skyscraper. Her honey-colored hair was even shinier when the sun's rays touched it, though the rays, enthralled by the young woman's beauty, seemed to caress her face with a certain tenderness. He was kneeling in front of her and holding a red velvet box inside which was a heart-shaped pendant with the letter "W" engraved in the center. For a moment the world around them seemed to stop, as though it wanted to watch the young lovers as their eyes exchanged dream-tinged promises of love. In a pause imbued with a sense of expectancy, he said, "Together, beyond the bounds of emotions."

The vision of Beatrice disappeared just as the sound of thunder made him jump and brought him back to reality.

He put his hand to his forehead as if struck by an intuition, and he thought again of his father's words in the video at the Eversten, the old movie theater: "I was sure that I needed to see a brain specialist because I kept having vivid hallucinations, but then I discovered that these were fragments of memories. The serum deprived me of the best memories of my life, and especially the emotions connected to them," and then, "…without my knowing it, they administered further doses of Em 0. I don't know how they did it…" Right then, he also remembered what Stuart had said at the Contempt City cemetery, "They appear to be administering the serum to you in some way. I don't know how but they are. If you have ever had a vivid hallucination you know what I'm talking about… they were not hallucinations; they're the real memories of your life!"

He felt confused and tried to organize the facts he had. At his birth, the doctors had administered Em 0, as they did to all newborns. Obviously, it did not have full effect on him, so during adolescence, most likely at school, the teachers noticed that he was able to express emotions on his face. These emotions had led him to fall in love with Beatrice and to share experiences with her like gazing into each other's eyes at the top of the skyscraper. The men from MC, aware of his ability to experience emotions, had given him additional doses of Em 0, though William, like his father Virgilio, did not remember ever receiving an injection.

And if Beatrice had shared experiences with him in the past, she must retain some memory of them. With great caution, he might talk with her about this.

Dr. Paul Shelton Malthen had succeeded in creating a vaccine to fight a very dangerous virus, capable of spreading rapidly and killing billions of people, but then he had also developed the Em 0 serum that could inhibit emotions. He had added the serum to the vaccine and administered it, with the government's complicity, to billions of people and all newborns. The doctors themselves were unaware of the fact that the vaccine had been mixed with a serum that erased emotions, and they continue to inject it to this day without problem. Dr. Paul and his son David in this way managed to control the world by means of their pharmaceutical company. But there was still another detail to work out. Not long ago, he had seen the video of a wedding where his mother appeared next to Dr. Paul Shelton Malthen. Maybe Madeline was a member of Emosemvi and had been taking part in the wedding in order to gather useful information for the resistance. She had to have been part of the resistance because in the video she had sent a coded message referring to the bride and groom, saying, "I wish Tom and Lara all the best. Today we are celebrating love. Look how sweet they are."

Little by little, he was making sense of the clues he had. Soon all the pieces of the puzzle would be in place, at which point he would confront David Shelton Malthen. He had to be careful though for he was a very influential, astute, and dangerous adversary.

Right then, William's thoughts turned to Beatrice. When he thought of her, he felt a curious sense of wellbeing; his heart pounded and his breathing sped up, clearly unusual physiological reactions. He understood that the strange feeling that could confuse a person, making them suffer and feel joy at the same time, was love.

Since he was a boy, he had liked to write in his spare time. Now that he could feel emotions, his writing was far better than before. It was as if he had learned to discern the nuances of color in the world. With words, he managed to describe the magic contained in the instant that comes before dawn or the poetry in the blossoming of a life. Love still existed in human beings, but it was buried beneath an impenetrable pall of frozen emotions.

Inspired by such thoughts, he wanted to try and capture emotions by writing a short piece for Beatrice, jotting it down on a scrap of paper:

> The fragile memories of our life are fragments of a timeless past, reflections of a lost love.

If you will, we could draw our destiny on the canvas of our days, painting the future in deep, emotive colors.

There is no fear where happiness shines; no surprise can make the heart waver of one who seeks the truth.

As he was putting the final touches to the lines, the trill of his cell phone interrupted him. "Will, it's John!"

"Hi, don't tell me you work even on Sundays!"

"Yeah, I'm working, and there's no time to waste. Meet me at Marleyes in Surprise City. I've got something to show you."

"OK, I'm on my way."

He went back down from the roof of the skyscraper and before getting into his car bought a hot coffee from a street vendor. Sipping the dark drink was something of a ritual, a bit of an affectation to pay homage to his Italian origins. It was from his grandfather Walter that he had inherited his practicality and his ability to solve problems in any situation, as well as the tendency to get a bit out of sorts when he had to follow rules.

He set off for Surprise City. By now the rain was falling heavily and covering everything in the world with its liquid mantle. When he reached his destination, he saw several police cars with flashing lights parked in a horseshoe formation outside Marleyes. John came over to meet him, exclaiming, "About time! Come and see what we've got here."

"What's happened?" asked William in a worried voice.

The two men stopped beside the dead body of a man lying on the ground with his face covered in a sheet. It was George, the owner of Marleyes and Stan's father.

"I feel bad for him. He didn't even get the chance to hug his son again. So many sad things have been happening lately," said William gloomily.

John took his arm and drew close to his ear and whispered, "Be careful what you say. There are agents around. Remember never to refer to emotions or there'll be trouble."

William nodded and winked at his colleague to indicate that he'd gotten the message. Forensics had put forward an initial theory about the cause of death: George had been poisoned. John pulled a latex glove onto his right hand and, rummaging in the dead man's jacket pockets, found a piece of paper with the symbol of the white mask with the three red tears just below the holes for the eyes and the numerical code: "MC = 13 - 1 - 4 – 5."

Looking at the piece of paper, John said, "The two initials are those of Minedal-e Corporation. Our friend George was clearly a member of the resistance. But what do the numbers mean? Maybe it's a code to open a safe."

"Or it could be the access code to a computer procedure," William suggested. "I don't know, I have to think about it. Let me take a picture of the number sequence."

"OK, Will, but be quick, because it's a piece of evidence and must be examined back at the station."

Soon afterward, John left the crime scene to go first to the police station and then home to get some rest. In a couple of days, the forensics team would have written the report, at which point Richard McMillan would give the officers instructions on how to proceed with the investigation.

William went back home, took a shower, copied down the code John had found in George's pocket onto a piece of paper, and hung it on the living room wall. The numbers made no sense at all, but in all likelihood deciphering them would allow the resistance to damage Minedal-e Corporation.

Someone rang the doorbell to announce they were at the door William went to open it and stood there speechless. It was Beatrice, beautiful as ever, and, with a touch of irony, she exclaimed, "I'm here to conduct a social experiment!"

If William had been able to allow himself the luxury of showing his emotions he would have burst into laughter. He felt he loved Beatrice even if her face was always an inexpressive blank. "Come on in, then. Actually, I need to talk with you."

Beatrice walked into the apartment and looked around a bit. In the kitchen, there was a basket full of dirty clothes, on the table, a shaky pile of empty cans that would soon be rolling all over the floor, and some congealed tomato sauce was sitting on the stove. In the living room were piles of books scattered around, and there and the curtains needed washing. William hurriedly picked up some balls of paper from the floor, exclaiming, "I was just cleaning up!"

"As I told you, I am here to conduct a social experiment. I would like to demonstrate how in an apartment belonging to a single man there is more dust than on an old country road. Judging by the work needed to clean up this place, I think you'll need quite a while. If you like I can come back in a year or two."

"No, no, make yourself comfortable. I've nearly finished tidying. The other rooms are already done."

Beatrice sat on a chair. The video camera hidden in the statue's eye by the fireplace was still active and recording the scene. William liked Beatrice's ironic manner of speech, as if she were trying to make him laugh, even though she couldn't feel emotions.

"Listen, I have to talk to you. It might seem strange, but..." William began hesitantly and with a trace of embarrassment.

Beatrice interrupted him brusquely, "Yeah, it does seem strange. At night it seems strange to dream of our wedding and my ivory gown. It's strange to see the two of us at the top of a skyscraper with you on one knee in front of me. And then I often feel a strange sensation around my chest. I think I need psychological counseling. Actually, sorry, I shouldn't be telling you all this. You must think I'm crazy. I shouldn't have come."

"There are so many things I have to explain to you, but now is not the time, or I'd be putting your life at risk. I've had the same hallucinations as you, and it can't be a coincidence, can it? We should actually call them memories and not hallucinations. In the past, we loved each other, but for some reason neither of us has clear memories of what happened to us."

"Well then, this is the perfect time to talk about it. I have a right to know what's happening to me!"

"All right, Beatrice. I'll tell you an incredible story, but you might have trouble believing it. Many years ago, a well-known pharmaceutical company, Minedal-e Corporation, distributed a vaccine containing a serum to inhibit the emotions of human beings. Then they started to inject newborn babies with it too. Some people like me, my father and now I think you too, are somewhat resistant to the serum and continue to feel emotions though somewhat toned-down. They drive us to do things, such as kissing passionately and running breathlessly and then laughing our heads off. But no sooner does the pharmaceutical company become aware of what is going on than it re-administers the serum to the individuals that show resistance. Besides inhibiting emotions in them again, it somehow also erases the memories tied to them."

"I can hardly believe it."

"I found it hard at first, too, to understand what actually happened. Once all human beings had emotions every day of their lives, and the world was very different than it is now. For example, today almost no one makes movies, but once they were very popular, and actors were really good at simulating the various states of mind."

"Sure, I see," said Beatrice, "and then aliens visiting earth steal our seawater through atomic straws, right? Yeah, William, your story really does sound pretty imaginative!"

William gave a loud laugh, and she was stunned because she couldn't remember ever having seen anyone laugh before in her life.

"Please, I'm dying laughing! I was imagining an alien drinking through an atomic straw!"

"Are you feeling OK? Why are you dying? Do you need a doctor?" asked Beatrice.

"No, I'm not dying. It's just an old expression that means: you've made me laugh a lot. Let's get back to serious things. I saw you a while ago in my first hallucination. You were sitting on a bench, wearing a long pink dress, and around your neck was the pendant that I gave you at the skyscraper."

"I've had that hallucination too!" she exclaimed. At that point, William went up to Beatrice and taking her hand and looking her in the eye, kissed her impulsively. But she drew back quickly, touching her chest, and cried, "My heartbeat has sped up, but I'm not running right now! What's happening to me?"

"This emotion is happiness, and it's often associated with the particular feeling called love," whispered William.

Beatrice stared at him for a moment, then she said she needed to be alone to get her mind straight. She thanked him for the hospitality and for telling her such a strange story then she left his apartment, closing the door behind her.

He stood looking at the front door, and just then he felt an intense sadness. As every emotion has a specific function needed for the survival of human beings, he didn't try to struggle against it, but let it flow freely until the emotional state in which he found himself brought to mind an idea: he would get hold of a dose of Reversing for Beatrice! Maybe if they experienced emotions together, their memories would return revealing important details about their past life.

William spent the next day at the police station, and as soon as he got to the end of his shift, he jumped on his motorcycle to ride over to Marleyes. It was the only place to find out how to get hold of Reversing, and it was also one of the few undercover resistance places not yet razed to the ground.

1.1

Fall was fast approaching, and the crisp evening air thrilled his heart. The sky was clear, and, on the way, William let his gaze wander freely, losing itself in the vastness of the horizon. Who knows what the sky would have said to humankind if it had the gift of speech? People were definitely bizarre because though they had everything needed to live, they were never satisfied. Humanity could learn a good deal more from nature. A cloud, for instance, was made from water, it lived its brief life gliding through the sky and stretching out while driven along by the wind and finished its days without much protest. Falling back down to earth again in the form of raindrops, it altruistically nourished the cycle of life by allowing its sisters to go up to the sky. Human beings, on the other hand, exploited the natural resources to the point of exhausting them completely, savagely polluting the planet with little care for the future. His mind occupied by these thoughts, he got to Marleyes.

He left the motorcycle right outside the restaurant, no light came from inside and it seemed deserted. At the height of the main entrance's door handle, there was a chain whose ends passed inside through two holes. William gave it a tug and it came off without much difficulty; it obviously hadn't been padlocked on the other side. He went into the restaurant and turned on his flashlight, there was transparent plastic sheeting hanging from the ceiling and various ink containers scattered around the floor, and in a corner were some buckets of colored paint. "The walls of the restaurant had recently been painted white, so what were the buckets of colored paint for?" he wondered as he turned on the flashlight. Suddenly, a noise very like that of a cogwheel echoed on the air. William spun around in the direction of the sound, but before he had even fully turned his face a light blinded him. A second later he was hit by a piece of metal piping on the nape of his neck and the room went dark.

He was out for a long time and when he opened his eyes, he found a light pointed at his face and his hands tied together with rope. There was someone standing in the darkness, and he spoke first. "Why are you here?"

"I'm looking for answers."

"This is the worst place to look for answers! Sorry, but now I'll have to kill you."

As William realized that he had very little hope of surviving, it occurred to him that the only chance he had was to try and use the code language of the resistance, so he said, "Really, the only person who is sorry is me given that I'm the one who is going to die, right?"

"I despise people like you; you're all the same. You think you know everything about the world, but you've never truly lived, and you've missed the best of life," said the stranger.

"Think whatever you like, but I'm not afraid of dying and if you really have decided to kill me then get on with it. Listen, I work for the police. A while ago I met George here who said he didn't know what had happened to his son Stan. My badge is in my coat. You can check if you like."

"The police is controlled by those criminals at Minedal-e. Why should I trust you? The fact that you are a cop gives me no guarantee of your integrity."

William sighed deeply. He might be someone from Emosemvi, or one of the operatives sent by Shelton Malthen trying to mislead him by pretending to despise Minedal-e. But the man expressed himself using emotions, so he knew the resistance code.

"I am disgusted by the very mention of that pharmaceutical company," added William in an irritated tone.

The light was turned on in the room and he saw a man with a familiar face, blond hair, brown eyes, and a small scar on his chin. He looked at him for a moment and then cried out, "Stan! Is that you?"

"How did you recognize me?"

"My colleague John and I went to talk to your father, and he showed us a photo of you. He was clearly worried because you had disappeared."

"My father's dead. He was a really good person and an honest worker. He wasn't greedy for money. He just wanted to give me the chance to live happily as a free man. But who can really feel free in a world without emotions? There's no point watching a football game anymore or having a beer with friends. And the worst sadness is in the empty expressions on people's faces. It might seem strange, but it's the truth."

"I agree with you, Stan, and I'm sorry about your father. I knew him, and he was a good guy. George had a code noted down on a piece of paper in his pocket. Can you tell me what it was?"

"No, unfortunately, I don't know anything about a code. The resistance assigns us jobs to do and sometimes we can't even tell our families the details."

"My father Virgilio was in the resistance. I know what it's like to lose a parent."

"Virgilio isn't a common name. Do you happen to be the son of Virgilio Pattern?"

"You knew my father?"

Stan untied the ropes around his wrists and replied, "Not personally, but my father told me a lot about him. Once the world was full of hate, people argued with each other and even ended up killing one another. War and pollution were the greatest problems, and no one knew which of the two would be first to lead humanity to extinction. Then Em 0 appeared, violence ceased, and the earth's pollution fell drastically. Of course, life is good without acts of violence, but in the resistance, we want to give every human being the chance to choose whether to do good or bad. Freedom is in choice!"

William listened to his words attentively, while the desire in him grew to hear more about his father's life.

Stan went on, "Virgilio was a biologist, and he worked at Minedal-e Corporation with your mother. He had a gift in that now and then he was able to feel emotions, but only in a muted way. One day your father was working in a laboratory at MC, when by chance there was a blackout, so he went to a nearby room to turn on the emergency generator. While he was fiddling with the generator, he saw two security guards from Minedal-e dragging an unconscious man by his arms. If I remember rightly the man's name was Ronald Inklings and he ran a café with his family in Sadness City."

"Incredible. That's the Somtlose. It's the café that blew up long ago. Tisiphone was Ronald's sister and she's dead too!" William cried.

"I know," said Stan shaking his head and adding, "Virgilio decided to follow them until he saw them disappear behind a sliding door into a restricted area. To gain access you had to have a special badge, but he didn't have one, so he stole a badge from the laboratory manager."

"Incredible!" exclaimed William.

"Exactly, but that's not all," continued Stan vehemently. "Once he entered the restricted area, he found the interrogation room and witnessed a truly sad sight. The man was tied to a chair and he was crying, and the two operatives asked him some questions and he showed that he felt anger, disgust, and contempt, in short, lots of emotions.

"I can imagine what they did to him."

"Yes, they injected a substance from a vial into his neck, and Ronald seemed to be calmed all of a sudden, and his anger vanished in a flash. Virgilio had seen enough and returned to his workstation. Over the following days, he did some research until in an archive he found the formula for Em 0, then he discovered that the serum was made in large quantities both in a building at Minedal-e and in a secret laboratory located on another continent."

"Which continent?"

"I don't know exactly, William."

"Anyway, the Em 0 was distributed throughout the world and administered mainly to newborn babies, but also to the individuals who, despite having already received a dose, for some reason showed that they could still feel emotions. Your father left Minedal-e Corporation and set up a team of experts to develop an antidote that could eliminate the effects of Em 0. After several failed attempts, they finally succeeded in developing Reversing and in freeing many people, until one day he decided to found Emosemvi and become its head. That is all my father told me, and I don't know anything more. Oh, wait! I remember something else: your father was killed by David Shelton Malthen himself."

William felt a stabbing pain in his chest, his heart began to thump hard. He clenched his fists and held his silence, then in a voice trembling with rage he said, "So my father didn't die in a car accident!"

"No, definitely not. I'm sorry, it's terrible to lose a father, I understand. If we don't stop Shelton Malthen, our fathers will have died in vain! The men from Minedal-e have discovered our network and are killing us all. This is where we print the promotional material. You'll no doubt have noticed the containers of ink at the entrance."

"I was wondering what the things strewn all over the floor were for," William confirmed.

Stan was visibly shaken after being reminded of the father to whom he had been so close; he paused briefly and sat down. In an attempt not to be overwhelmed by growing sadness, he took a deep breath and went on, "Once my father used to run a print shop with a colleague named Johannes in a place called Magonza. One of the resistance leaders named Jacqueline helped them print the promotional material. While they were printing 1468 flyers with the resistance slogan, "The cure is in emotions. Don't be made to conform." MC raided the print shop and confiscated all the promotional material. My father and Jacqueline managed to get away, but Johannes died that day."

"I didn't know the resistance was so well organized, Stan."

"Sure was, and the credit goes to Virgilio, your father, though since his death things have changed and sad to say, not for the better. Here at the restaurant, we have continued to print material secretly for Emosemvi. A while ago we were printing some posters when two men turned up at the door saying they were policemen. They roped my hands together and threw me in the back of a van. Unfortunately for them, I had a utility knife in my pocket, and I managed to cut the rope and quickly throw myself out of the moving van. I didn't know where to go so I hid at a friend's house for a few days."

"You can't say anything to the police. Stay hidden, but not here because it's dangerous. I'm looking for a vial of Reversing. Do you know where I can find one?" asked William, with a hopeful look.

"It's getting harder and harder to find Reversing, but today is your lucky day because I've got some here." Stan put on a plastic glove, went over to a can of paint, and sunk his hand into the paint until he found what he was looking for. He pulled out a plastic bag covered in paint that he rinsed under the tap, then he drew out a vial and handed it to William, saying, "Do you know how it works?"

"Yes, thanks. Now let's get away from this place. I'm sure we'll meet again in the future. For now, I owe you one. Good luck!"

"Let's hope next time we meet in a free world."

William left Marleyes with a crashing headache because of the blow to his head. He went back to his apartment, quickly made a plate of pasta for dinner, then sat holding a bag of ice to his head and mulling over recent events.

2. The awakening

William knocked on Beatrice's door, but she didn't seem to be at home. After a bit, she came to the door and without opening it she asked him to go away because she needed time to think. He sat on the floor outside her door and stayed there for many hours. Then, when it was late at night, Beatrice came back to the door again. "Are you still there?"

"Yes, I need to talk with you about something very important. Come on, open the door."

"Please give me time to think. I need to understand what's happened. Out of the blue, my neighbor tells me that he is my husband, or at least so it seems from a dream or a hallucination we've both had. And the world is not as I know it because someone has been having fun removing emotions from human beings. Other than that, everything's just smooth sailing over here."

"Together, beyond the bounds of emotions!"

"What did you say, William?"

"Do you remember when I said that to you? We were at the top of a skyscraper, and you looked so beautiful."

Beatrice opened the door and stood back to let him in. "You've got two minutes, and then I'm going to bed."

"I only need one, don't worry. I've managed to get hold of some Reversing."

William pulled the vial of serum out of his pocket. "If you take this you will be able to go back to feeling emotions and little by little, you'll… we'll get back our memories."

"No way I'd even consider it. First, you upset my life telling me a story that verges on the unbelievable. Then, as if that's not enough, you turn up at my door with a vial of I don't know what and expect me to inject myself with it, without even knowing if my body will reject it or if there will be side effects. How do I know this serum won't kill me? What pharmaceutical company makes it anyway? No, hang on, I know, it's the Science Fiction Corporation, isn't it?"

William smiled and stroked her cheek. "All right, I'll go. Just as I came into your life, I'll leave it, quietly. At any rate, you won't suffer because you can't feel sadness, can you? Nothing's going to change at all. There's no point in finding out what is outside your front door. Tomorrow morning as you look at yourself in the mirror you'll find, like every other day, that you have a face with no expression. In a few years, you'll marry a man with a heart as cold as ice, and you'll bring children into the world who will receive an injection and, from that exact moment on, their lives will be changed forever because they'll never again be able to smile."

"Your imagination is running wild..."

He did not let her finish the sentence and continued, "I dream of a world that's different from the one we have today, one where children run home from school into the arms of their parents. I want to see children playing in the parks and laughing like crazy. I want to cry at a funeral and dedicate my tears to the person who has died. I want to hug a friend who is happy because something has gone well in his life and support him when times are hard, suffering with him. I dream of an imperfect world, one that isn't equal, but where everyone has the opportunity to choose to do good or bad."

Beatrice stood in silence for a moment, then looking him in the eye, she said, "I don't agree. I have a job and a nice apartment. The world is fine with me just as it is. I don't need to change anything in my life."

Without saying a word, William left her apartment, slamming the door behind him. He went home, sent an email to John telling him that the next day he wouldn't be going in to work. Then worn out by exhaustion he fell asleep on the couch.

The following morning, his mind full of thoughts, he lay staring at the living room ceiling for a while and then turned on the television. The news was still covering the stories of people mysteriously disappearing. The journalists had apparently also been corrupted by the pharmaceutical company because none mentioned the strangeness of all those sudden disappearances.

In the evening someone knocked on his door. Tired and discouraged, William went to open it and his eyes widened in amazement: there stood Beatrice with her usual inexpressive face, but lovely as ever. "I thought about it all night, William. Then I looked out of the window, but it's always the same view. I don't want to go through the rest of my life and regret not seeing the world from another perspective. Together, beyond the bounds of emotions!"

He hugged her tight, then prepared the syringe and injected her with Reversing. "You've got an hour to experience all seven basic emotions, otherwise, the effect of the Reversing will vanish. The first changes will already be obvious after a few hours, then emotions will gradually start to appear. Your facial muscles will wake up and you will be able to express emotions. Remember never to show any emotion when you're in a public place, or you'll risk being killed by the men from Minedal-e."

Beatrice nodded and closed her eyes, and then after apologizing, William slapped her across the face. Her eyes widened as she felt the emotion of surprise, then she was noticeably angry and slapped him back. "That's a great start!" she cried.

Taking her by the hand, he led her down to the street. A homeless man was asleep on a bench under some flattened cardboard boxes, and William turned to Beatrice asking her to look at him and express the emotions she felt. She answered that she felt sadness but as she spoke her face remained inexpressive. He asked her to wait a moment because he needed to buy something and disappeared into a nearby clothing store. He returned carrying a bag from which he pulled a wool coat. He handed it to Beatrice and asked her to give it to the homeless man. She went up to the man covered in cardboard from whom there actually came an unpleasant smell. As the expression of disgust appeared on her face, she said shyly, "Excuse me, I thought you might like this coat to keep the cold out."

The homeless man took the wool coat and thanked her. He said that he had never received such a kind gesture since he'd had to live on the streets. Beatrice's face assumed the form of sadness. Even though the homeless man had lived on the bench opposite her apartment for some time, she had never once spoken a word to him or offered him any kind of help. Upset, she promised herself she would come back in the future with some food for him and maybe even a gift of new clothes. Time was moving quickly, and William asked her to follow him to the curb of the sidewalk. The cars were roaring by and it was definitely not a good time to cross the street, but he took her hand and began to run across, dodging the cars. Beatrice was terrified she was going to be knocked down and felt intense fear, then when they were both safely on the other side of the street, she shouted full of contempt, "You're crazy! I was nearly killed!"

William kissed her and right at that long-awaited moment, the two young sweethearts shared the emotion of happiness.

They went back to Beatrice's apartment as she was feeling a strange sleepiness due to the side effect of the serum. Now she just needed to rest. Soon they would be able to be together to try to re-evoke memories and reconstruct their past. He left her at her place and went home happy and satisfied. That evening William read the psychology book again to find out more about certain concepts relating to the functioning of emotions, body language and facial expressions. Then with a smile fixed on his face he fell asleep, dreaming of love.

The next day he went into the police station and met John, who thanks to the report made by forensics could make his own report and confirm poisoning as the cause of George's death. William chose not to say anything to him about meeting Stan at Marleyes.

He spent the day at the station filling in forms and putting in order all the documents relating to the case of George's death. It was late, night had fallen, and all his colleagues had left. A noise suddenly caught his attention and he leaned out of his cubicle to find out the source of it. A man in an untamed beard, with long white hair and a red uniform from "Aegi," the cleaning company he worked for, was polishing a desk with a cloth. His name was Tim, and William remembered having seen him before. It had been a while ago when McMillan and William had met by the elevator doors and Tim had seemed to want to listen in on their conversation. On that occasion, Tim had frowned for a fraction of a second, as if he were able to feel the emotion of anger. William had noticed the expression briefly appearing on his face, but at the time he had given it no importance. "You must be Tim, if I'm not mistaken. We've met here before."

"Yes, I've been working here for many years, sir."

"Let's get straight to the point. Tell me if you are a member of the resistance."

"I am not a member of the resistance, and I don't know what you're talking about."

As he said these words, Tim raised his right shoulder for a fraction of a second, so William decided to take advantage of the newly-learned notions about body language that had so fascinated him in his studies. "The asymmetric lifting of a shoulder is an emblematic movement. Did you know that?"

"Sorry, sir?"

"As you were stating that you are not a member of the resistance, you raised your right shoulder, which means that you are not convinced by what you are saying. It's possible to lie with words but more difficult to lie with the body. Now can you tell me if you are in the resistance?"

"I wasn't aware of making any movement, and, as I said, I don't know what you're talking about."

While repeating himself, Tim rubbed his nose and William pressed him, "One of the most common gestures revealing a sense of annoyance is rubbing the nose. The erectile tissue in the nasal cavity is linked by means of a series of connections to the amygdala, which translates a psychological annoyance into a sensorial one. So if you are now feeling a sense of annoyance, I only have to go on asking you questions to stimulate anger in you."

Tim took a step back while for less than a second his forehead contracted, making his eyebrows converge downwards together.

"You took a step back. This is referred to as a gestural retreat. You are finding the conversation uncomfortable and would like to leave, and furthermore, a micro-expression of anger appeared on your face for less than a second. Now, Tim, you can stop pretending and make it all easier, OK?"

"OK, off with the mask. Emosemvi assigned me the task of contacting you, but I was supposed to wait for another couple of months. Let's say we've jumped the gun a bit. Now listen. Right now, lots of places associated with the resistance are being blown up, the owners are disappearing with no trace or are brutally killed. Somehow the men from MC have discovered and tracked our network."

Tim picked up a bottle of floor cleaner and pressed down as if to open it, at which point a secret compartment sprang open. He pulled out a sort of remote control with a single button in the center and a piece of paper with a code written on it: "12N - 9 - 14 - 050E." Then he said, "This remote control locates bugs and electronic devices hidden in a room or in the folds of clothing. You just have to point it at a wall or an object and if it makes a long beep it means there is a working electronic device there. Use it with care and, most importantly, check to see if the Minedal-e operatives have paid a visit to your apartment to install bugs. The numbers on this piece of paper are the second part of a code. I don't know how to decipher it. I have merely been ordered to hand it over to you and tell you that your mother is alive. The code will lead you to her."

William felt a shiver run down his spine.

"The first part of the code will be given to you by another member of the resistance by the name of George, the owner of Marleyes restaurant in Surprise City. He will explain how to decipher the code," Tim concluded hurriedly."

"Unfortunately George died, but I managed to get the code anyway."

"Goddamn it! They killed him!"

William grabbed a chair and leaned on the back to hold himself up. He was speechless, if Madeline was still alive why hadn't she ever tried to contact him? Maybe his mother was the head of the resistance and couldn't risk the luxury of having a family. He had to find her! And it was also time to bring an end to the Shelton Malthen dynasty! As he was reflecting on this, Tim said, "Now I have to go. My job here is done. The security cameras will certainly have filmed us. This wasn't the way I was planning to contact you, but in life not everything goes according to plan. Now I have to lie low for a while. Government agents and Shelton Malthen's men could already be at my place. Goodbye."

He put the bottle with the secret compartment back in his cart, next to a photo of a girl in a plastic frame. There was a dedication on it, "I love you, Dad, your Claire." Tim walked quickly to the door. William didn't have time for more questions, let alone to inform him of George's death. His heart was full of hope, and he couldn't wait to embrace his mother! "So she hadn't died the day I was born, perhaps her cover had been blown, MC was after her, and the resistance had decided she should be out of the picture" he though.

He was doing his best to control his emotions because in the space of a short time he had found out the truth about both his father and his mother. It was as though a veil woven with the thread of deceit had fallen from his eyes.

2.1

When he got home, even before taking off his coat, William took the bug detector out of his pocket and started to point it around. First, he pointed it into the kitchen, but nothing happened, and then at the chimney in the living room and there was a long beep. He walked over to take a closer look at the statues at the side of the chimney, but there were no apparent signs of tampering. The only strange thing was a tiny drop of glue on one of the eyes; using a knife he pried off the top layer of marble and realized that it fell apart too easily, so he applied more pressure until the lens of a tiny video camera came out of its nook and fell to the floor.

How long had it been there? A while ago, the place had been turned upside down by thieves. Presumably the attempted theft was only a cover-up for the installation of the video camera by Shelton Malthen's men. William opened his eyes wide and put his hand to his forehead as though he had been hit by an insight, then he rushed out of his apartment and over to Beatrice's. As the door was ajar, he pulled out his pistol and went in, the place was in chaos with clothes strewn everywhere, but there was no sign of Beatrice. The men from Minedal-e must have overheard the recent conversation between him and Beatrice in his apartment and thanks to the video camera now they even knew about the existence of Reversing. William had unintentionally supplied a great deal of information to the enemy. The resistance would be wiped out and he felt responsible for it.

Back in his apartment, he called John to tell him about the hidden video camera and the disappearance of Beatrice. John acted as only a true friend could. He advised him not to report her disappearance because the police station was overrun with spies. Meanwhile, he would immediately do what he could to find Beatrice. William thanked him warmly, said goodbye and started to consider his next move.

Almost by chance, his eye fell on the piece of paper tacked up on the living room wall with the code found in George's jacket. He copied it down onto a piece of paper and then added the other part of the code that he had gotten from Tim at the police station, creating a single string of numbers: MC = 13 - 1 - 4 - 5 -12N - 9 - 14 - 050E. "What do these numbers mean? Maybe, like John had suggested, it's a code to open a safe," he thought, trying to concentrate.

He sat staring at the numbers for hours, tried inverting the numerical order, copying them down differently, and adding them up, but nothing seemed to work; gradually all hopes of deciphering the code seemed to vanish like a bubble of soap. He lay on the couch and let his gaze wander around the room as if he could find the necessary inspiration to break the code in one of the objects around him.

Nothing occurred to him for hours until finally he was staring at a large book on a shelf with the title "Exploring with the Atlas." Leaping to his feet he exclaimed, "Coordinates! They are geographic coordinates!" He ran over to the computer and typed: 13°14'51.2"N 9°14'05.0"E. On the screen appeared satellite images of a place in the desert of Niger, in Africa. The code found on George's dead body was not made up only of a numerical sequence, but also the acronym MC, or rather that of Minedal-e Corporation.

William wondered what his mother could be doing at a branch of the pharmaceutical company; maybe she had been identified as a member of the resistance and arrested. "She must be being held against her will in an underground construction because the satellite images were of a desert area devoid of buildings" he told himself.

He was worried about Beatrice, and he also had to find a way of joining his mother to rescue her too. The shrill ring of the telephone cut through the quiet in the room, bouncing off the living room walls. It was John and he had good news. He was calling on a secure line from the office so that no one would be able to trace the call or listen in on the conversation. Beatrice was alive, but the men from Minedal-e had kidnapped her; to rescue her they would have to go to an Emosemvi meeting and ask for help from the members of the resistance. The next day William should go to a public park in Anger City where a trusted person would approach him to reveal the meeting place. William thanked John sincerely, in the end, he could always count on him, he was also the only friend with whom he could speak freely and express his emotions.

William didn't shut an eye all night. Dr. Shelton Malthen had destroyed his life, but the time had come to make him pay for it. In the morning, after a quick breakfast and a refreshing shower, he dressed, checked that his pistol was loaded and slipped it into its holster; then he went to the living room and opened the wooden panel of the grandfather clock; he turned the hands counter-clockwise until a secret wooden door opened at its base. He took out a small pistol. It was light and once he had loaded the magazine, he placed it in the holster that he tied around his ankle. In case of danger, extra firepower might save his life.

As he went downstairs, he thought back to what he had learned from Leonardo at the academy. The day after taking part in a pistol training session at the firing range, they were in class for a theory lesson. The students were being shown one of the few videos still in circulation of an armed robbery that had happened a long time before, in which you could see a criminal disarm a security guard. As the video images filled the screen, in the dark of the room, William heard someone say his name. Leonardo told him that the armed robbery would not have been successful if the security guard at the bank had kept a second pistol in an ankle holster.

"First of all, no one robs banks these days, and a second pistol isn't any use anyway," replied William quietly.

144

"That's what you think! You never know what situations you might find yourself in. The world might change again. What'll happen if one day human beings start feeling emotions again and start to fight each other? Better to be prepared. I wouldn't waste a chance to stay alive. As a matter of fact, as soon we finish at the academy, I'm going to buy an extra pistol, and I'll even give it a name."

"You want to give a pistol a name, Leo?"

"Yes, I'm going to call it Second Chance."

They couldn't continue with the conversation because the teacher called for silence.

William shook his head and then he smiled to think of the episode and his friend Leonardo. He should give him a call to find out how he was, but right now there was no time for that.

He jumped onto the motorcycle and rode out of the garage despite the fact that the weather wasn't perfect. Fall was around the corner and the morning air was pretty cold. Anger City was a decidedly beautiful city, though it did seem a bit run down, and on every street corner there were machines and men at work. It looked like an open-air building site. Having reached the public park at Anger City, he sat down on a bench to wait for his contact. A man in an elegant suit and a hat came up. William rose to his feet and put out his hand, but the man passed by, making straight for the ice cream seller. Obviously, the well-dressed man was not his contact.

He sat on the bench again and stayed there until 1:00 p.m., when, tired of sitting there doing nothing, he decided to stretch his legs by taking a stroll towards the main street, at that very moment a couple of cars collided before his eyes. He ran to the scene of the accident to see if anyone was hurt. The drivers got out of their cars. One of them had knocked his head on the steering wheel and turned to the man who had driven into him, saying with an inexpressive face, "My car is ruined, and my head hurts," and the other man, in a calm tone, replied, "Yes, I was sending a message on my cell phone, and I got distracted."

William asked the injured man if he needed a doctor, but he answered no, he was going to call his insurance and then the police to report the accident. In the old world, those two men would have had an argument, while now they were talking quite calmly about the dynamics of the accident. William went back to his bench and kept on waiting, but the park was deserted and there was no sign of his contact.

After a while, he got up and went over to the ice cream seller. He was the only regular person in the park, maybe he was the Emosemvi contact. He bought an ice cream, and in the conversation, he tried to use the resistance code by asking him questions that contained words like "happiness" or "disgust," but the man's face remained impassive, obviously he really was just an ice cream seller. Meanwhile, the afternoon was hurrying towards evening, and a cool wind rustled the leaves of the trees lit by the last rays of the sun, almost seeming to blush shyly a bit more.

Some children came into the park with their parents, but the area with slides and swings didn't seem to interest them. They preferred to walk along and look about them, as though they couldn't find a game to play. In the old world, children loved to run and play carefree. Any stick or pebble could attract their attention and be imaginatively transformed into a sword or ammunition for a slingshot. Evening came and William was on the point of leaving. He had the feeling that he had wasted precious time. His mother and Beatrice were in danger while he was hanging around for someone who probably didn't even exist. He was getting back on his motorcycle when he heard someone calling him. He turned and saw a little boy, who asked, "Are you leaving, mister?"

"Yes, why?"

"Don't you like the park?"

"Yes, I do, but it's getting late, and I must go now."

"I love playing with my ball, but here I'm not supposed to, so I play in the courtyard at home where no one can see me."

William generally didn't mind talking with children, but after a long day sitting on a bench he wasn't in the right mood, so he tried to cut things short. "I'm glad you like playing ball. Are you here with your parents?"

"Yes, with my dad. He's over there though he's not very good company today because he's sad."

The child pointed to a man reading the paper on a bench.

"OK, now you go back to him and have some fun. What is the world other than a great big playground?"

William turned on the motorcycle's ignition and the child added in a shy voice: "Gear Jesture at 11:00 p.m. It's two blocks from here."

"Sorry, what?"

But the child didn't reply. He just turned and ran to join his father. Then the two of them quickly disappeared into the evening shadows just before the park lights came on. William stood there astonished; a child using the resistance code had just revealed the location of the meeting.

3. Like a secret Carbonari meeting

William decided to leave the motorcycle at the Anger City public park and walk to a nearby bar to get a sandwich. There weren't many people around, and the traffic was light at that hour. Such an unusual calm in the city did not presage well, seeming the classic hush before the storm with lightning flickered on the horizon.

He called John asking him to find a secure line and call him back. When he did, they arranged to meet at 10:50 p.m. outside Gear Jesture, a garage specialized in souping up engines for better performance.

He got to Gear Jesture on foot at the agreed time and found John waiting for him, wearing an unusual bright red hat. They greeted each other with a gesture but no words; a complicit glance said it all. Soon a man wearing a long brown coat with a fur collar knocked four times on the roller shutter to the garage. It opened and he went in, then it closed quickly behind him. William and John did the same, knocking four times, but the roller shutter didn't open. They

149

tried again and nothing happened. A video camera fixed to a lamppost next to the roller shutter was filming them. The small red dot of a laser beam wavered slightly at the level of William's chest; he was clearly in someone's sights. From inside the garage, they heard a loud ruckus, and somebody shouted, "It's him! Let him in!" The roller shutter opened and they were surrounded by at least ten people. Stan, George's son, came forward and said hello to William. "We meet again. Who's your friend?"

"Hi Stan, this is John, the colleague I was telling you about. Your father met him when you were lying low."

"OK, come on in."

The man in the long brown coat who had just arrived frisked them both, confiscating their pistols. Then he went to the center of the garage, inviting everyone to take one of the wooden seats arranged around a circular table. The people gathered for the meeting seemed very normal, each wearing the uniform of their day jobs; there were two janitors in red jumpsuits, a carpenter with sawdust in his hair and a pencil still stuck behind his ear, two nurses dressed in white, two farmers in checked shirts, one old and the other young and two fishermen wearing dark blue caps. The man in the coat with the fur collar seemed to be the wealthiest of the bunch.

There was a strong smell of motor oil in the air, two cars sitting in the corner with their hoods up, and a lot of mechanic's tools scattered around the place. It didn't seem a very secure place to hold a secret meeting because the garage only had one exit and high windows that had to be reached by ladder. The first to speak was Stan, "Friends of Emosemvi, welcome. Let's start our meeting with a minute's silence for members of the resistance who are no longer with us."

Just then, the carpenter began to cry. Stan went up to William and very quietly told him that recently the man's daughter had been poisoned while delivering a vial of Reversing to a friend. One of the fishermen put a hand on the carpenter's shoulder to console him. Stan waited a few minutes to allow the carpenter to collect himself, then he said, "I declare this meeting open. Here today we have the highest echelons of the resistance and we have important decisions to make. There are many matters to be discussed this evening, but first allow me to introduce John, a police officer, and William Pattern, son of the founder of the resistance Virgilio Pattern."

A deep silence fell on the garage as if someone had pulled out the plug of a stereo while the speakers were playing at full volume. One of the two farmers was an old man with shaggy hair, a pronounced nose and large hands, who used a sort of ear trumpet to hear better. He asked Stan to repeat his last sentence because he hadn't heard him properly. So raising his voice and going up to the farmer's ear trumpet, Stan said, "Tobias, this is Virgilio Pattern's son!"

The farmer nodded to show that he had understood and then turned to William exclaiming, "I knew your father! We met one day at my farm just outside Disgust City. He came saying his car had broken down. He had a large leather suitcase with him and told me that he didn't have much time because he had to drop off some medicine for a friend. Somehow, I knew I could trust him, so I decided to lend him the cart and my mare Bertha."

Stan made a hand gesture to Tobias to encourage him to keep it brief. In return, Tobias said, "Let me finish my story, son. Everything goes too fast in this world. People communicate with those electronic contraptions. Everyone is connected and yet they find themselves so goddamn alone!"

In a solemn tone, he continued his account. "Where was I… ah yes! Virgilio. Well, once he was in the cart and holding the reins, he said that thanks to me he would be able to free a lot of people that day. After saying the words, he smiled. At the time I didn't give it much thought, but after a few days when he brought back Bertha and the cart, he smiled at me again."

"Dad, don't start telling that story again. We've all heard it before. We have to get on with the meeting now," said the younger farmer going up to Tobias and speaking into his ear.

Tobias, taking no notice of his son, went on undaunted, "Our friends haven't heard it before. I'm the oldest here so I'll talk as much as I want. And so, William, that day your father gave me a new life because he injected me with Reversing. From that moment on, the world seemed brighter and more colorful. My life finally made sense. I was a different man! I also found I wanted to learn new things, when I got in from the fields I would even study literature. Amazing, isn't it?"

"It is!" Stan exclaimed.

The old man nodded and continued, "Then I became the courier for the resistance and when anyone needed a case of Reversing, I would load it onto my cart hiding it beneath the straw and deliver it to them. My wife Martha never wanted to inject any serum. She claimed that she did not need emotions because they made you suffer, and suffering was a terrible thing. One afternoon while I was working in the fields, the men from MC turned up at our farm and took Martha away with them, from that day on I never saw her again. Then the government seized our land, and Virgilio cried with me over this evil act."

Stan put a hand on old Tobias' shoulder, thanking him for sharing his memories with the others, then needing to move the meeting along, he said hurriedly, "Gentlemen, we are here this evening because we are losing our battle. I don't know how, but the operatives from Minedal-e are systematically locating and killing every member of the resistance. Today there should have been twenty-five Emosemvi associates in this room, and we are less than half that! The number of free people is falling drastically and if we go on at this rate, in about three months we won't have the strength to take on Shelton Malthen. Three of the five secret laboratories where we produce Reversing have been blown up, and it is becoming increasingly hard to get hold of the raw materials and, even more, to find personnel qualified to mix the substances to make up the serum."

The man with the brown coat rose to speak. He had a well-groomed look with well-brushed gray hair and there were deep, grooved lines on his face suggesting to the world that he had faced many difficulties in his lifetime. "For those who don't know me, my name is Romance, and I have belonged to the resistance for several years. I work in import-export at the port in Contempt City, running the firm Rotaon Ltd. Just for the record, the fur collar of this coat is synthetic, as I don't like killing animals, apart, of course, from those who work for MC. My job is a little like that of Tobias, though I don't use a cart."

Everyone laughed, Romance winked at Tobias, who raised a conspiratorial hand, then continued, "I can't understand how the people from Minedal-e are managing to identify all our people! Since every one of us is well trained and knows never to betray any emotion."

"Neither do I, but we must find out soon if we want to survive!" exclaimed Stan.

"The resistance needs a new leader and William is certainly the most suitable person," stated Tobias decisively. Then he turned to William. "Son, the time has come to continue the legacy of your father and lead the resistance to victory. Since he died, we've been doing our best in the name of freedom, but we no longer have a real leader. I suggest we put it to the vote, and if the majority of those here agree, you will lead us to safety. When Stan told us he had tracked you down, we couldn't believe it. I think your time has come, son!"

William sighed deeply. "Tobias, thank you for such moving words, I am grateful to everyone here for their contribution to Emosemvi, without you there would be no hope for the world or for the emotions of billions of people. I'm here this evening because Shelton Malthen's men have kidnapped both my mother and the woman I love. I need the help of your network of friends to gather information and find them both. In truth, I know where my mother is being held, but I've got to get there in total secrecy and without showing a passport at any border controls. In the end, I don't think I'm the right person to lead the resistance. I am not up to the task and there are other more qualified people than me, with more experience, who can make a better contribution to the cause."

"Virgilio's blood is running through your veins, and you are the right person to rebuild the Emosemvi network and to unite all of us under a single cause," insisted Tobias.

Then Romance took the floor again. "I agree with William! You need experience to lead the resistance. The position of leader cannot be handed down by some sort of dynastic right. Respect must be earned on the ground."

Tobias retorted, "He inherited the right from his father! Maybe it is true, oftentimes it would be better not to feel pain. I cried for the loss of my Martha until I had no tears left, but I suffered as a free man. Emotions are a gift of nature and should be appreciated. When you are used to feeling emotions, you aren't aware of how important they are, but it's just when you can't cry that you realize you have lost the most precious gift."

One of the two fishermen nodded in agreement with Tobias, who concluded with greater emphasis, "We must think of the generations to come, and without a leader, we have no chance of victory. We'll keep on losing our members because we are disorganized. We need a leader to change the world, and William is the right man, trust me!"

He had hardly finished speaking when the garage windows were blown to splinters, smoke bombs came sailing through them and before anyone could work out what was happening, the roller shutter at the entrance exploded. Stan threw himself to the ground and lifted up the edge of a rubber mat to reveal a trapdoor beneath. Minedal-e Corporation operatives in gasmasks were flooding into the garage, brandishing automatic rifles. At the same time Stan disappeared through the trapdoor and down a tunnel, William swiftly followed him, as did John and Romance.

They heard shots and yelling. Stan ran fast down the narrow underground passage, and the others ran behind. The air was scarce and there was no light. The voices of the Minedal-e operatives seemed to be coming closer. They had obviously found the trapdoor and were in pursuit. Stan lit a plastic fluorescent stick to light the way until they reached a small room with rough rock walls; there was no way out and it seemed to be a dead end. From under his coat, Romance pulled out John's pistol and those of William. "I was keeping these for you, now is the moment to use them, at least for one last time."

He handed the pistols to their rightful owners who prepared to use them with a glimmer of hope in their eyes.

Maybe this was the end of it all, they would die in that hole carved into the rock and no one would ever know. William thought of Beatrice, as he meant to dedicate his last breath to her and for a second, he had a vision of her wearing the ivory wedding gown, radiant with happiness, smiling at the future. He would have liked to spend the rest of his life with her, but just then every plan seemed to melt like snow in sunshine.

Stan surprised them all by removing a small wooden plank leaning horizontally against the bottom of the rock wall; behind it was a tiny burrow, so narrow that you couldn't even crawl along it. Stan lay down on a low platform with four wheels and pulled a rope that fastened the ends to two small pulleys. The platform carried him to the other end of the tunnel, the others followed suit. When they were all on the other side of the tunnel, Stan began to climb a ladder that went up to a manhole on the street, he pushed up the lid and they all climbed out into the open. Then he took a remote control out of his pocket and sent a radio signal to an explosive charge placed inside the tiny burrow they had just got through. The ground trembled under their feet and a rumble confirmed that the roof of the underground tunnel had caved in. Stan turned to his friends, "We must go in separate directions. We'll find a way to meet again. They'll be onto us in no time. Run!"

The men vanished into the night. Still covered in dirt, William reached his motorcycle, congratulating himself on his decision to park it a good distance from Gear Jesture, and then like a thunderbolt he sped home. When he got there, he pulled a heavy desk up to the front door to barricade himself in. His heart was still thumping fast, and the adrenalin in his body didn't seem to be diminishing. The risk of him being killed was high. Now he couldn't set foot in the police station again and not even his boss McMillan would be unable to protect him. He checked for the pistol in his hip holster and the other at his ankle. A "second chance" would definitely be useful right then. He quickly threw some clothes into a bag and ran down to the car.

4. Revelations

William drove around aimlessly. Unfortunately, he had nowhere to go. He could only trust John and Leonardo, and in a way, he felt responsible for ruining their careers by involving them in the fight against the pharmaceutical giant. If he could have gone back in time, he would definitely have fought his battle on his own, leaving them out of it. But it was impossible to re-write the past, he could only think of the future and trying to rescue Madeline and Beatrice.

Lost in these thoughts, he spotted a country road and turned into it, and he soon noticed an old ruined farmhouse sitting in the middle of a plowed field that was the perfect place to spend the night. To avoid being tracked down by the police communications specialists he had not turned on his cell phone. The next day he would find a way of getting in touch with John.

The farmhouse windows had peeling paint and broken panes, and part of the roof had collapsed, but some rooms, like the kitchen, were still intact. In the past, the country kitchen had been the center of the farmers' lives, was where they ate, told stories, and warmed up by the fire, the solitary witness of many family events. The great marble fireplace was still standing in the old kitchen, so William lit a fire to warm himself and then sat gazing into it for a while.

"It's wonderful to think of how fire, in its short life span, set free its ardent power and shared it with the world. Perhaps it's not very different from what happens in love. When two people first meet, they look at each other, then in an instant, the coolness of their glance is softened by the light of a shy spark, which can reach both hearts and ignite them with true passion," he thought as he pulled a piece of paper and a small pencil out of his pocket.

Inspired by the dance of the flames reflected on the wall and such thoughts, William composed a song for Beatrice and wrote it down on a piece of paper:

> The whisper of time is a reflection of the past, a moment of the present and the hope of a future dream.
> A night too dark for waiting, give me your hand to melt any doubts, light the way whispering my name, I will follow your voice, be near me.
> We will hold tight in our hands those dreams too great to speak to us of tomorrow, caresses of a desire without reality slip on the mirror of false truths.

We shall abandon that life of silences, to lose ourselves in the clamor of the world of differences, certainties that vanish for eternity, hopes that are born of a bitter truth.

Lulled by the words and his thoughts, he fell asleep in front of the fire in that isolated house in the countryside. The next day he was woken by the light of dawn, rubbing his eyes and looking around him. At first, he couldn't remember where he was, then he realized that he wasn't at home surrounded by his bedroom furniture, but by an old fireplace with the embers still warm, which with a puff of smoke seemed to want to greet the first light of morning. Then, like an overflowing river came the memories, and with them, the sadness, and then all the other emotions came like a herd of galloping horses.

Leaving the farmhouse, he rode to a motel and called John from an old payphone, and after a few rings he answered, "Yes."

"John?"

"Jeez, you're alive!"

"What happened, John?"

"It's all over the news. You've been accused of belonging to a criminal organization, and the police are looking for you. Shelton Malthen obviously had a word with his friends in the police to get them to hunt you down. Some men from the resistance work undercover for Minedal-e Corporation. One named Peter saw Beatrice in a cell near Shelton Malthen's office."

"We have to go and get her out of there!"

"Yes, but cool your jets, that place is swarming with guards. My contact at the pharmaceutical company will get us both workman's jumpsuits and counterfeit badges, which is the only way to get in and rescue Beatrice. See you in two hours in the parking lot near Anger City airport. Peter will be with me."

"OK, I'll be there and… John?"

"Yes?"

"Thanks, you're a real friend."

"We'll have time to celebrate. Friends always help each other."

William hung up the phone, his heart overwhelmed by hope because soon he would be with Beatrice! He got to Anger City airport earlier than scheduled, parked his car, and sat on a low wall in a secluded place from which he had a good view of the parking lot. John showed up on time with a different car from the one he usually drove. The police were probably after him too and he didn't want to arouse suspicion. In the car with him was Peter, a thin man with a thick red beard, an aquiline nose, and large square glasses. Behind the light-sensitive lenses, you could just make out a pair of small blue eyes lit up with a slight gleam. William went up to John who, after looking about to see if he was being caught on video camera, said, "You look good."

Indicating Peter with his hand, he went on, "This is Peter, he'll explain how we get into Minedal-e Corporation and he'll come in the car with us."

Peter waved in greeting. "Hi, William. John has told me a lot about you. I've brought two workmen's jumpsuits and two counterfeit badges. They've been perfectly copied so you'll have no trouble getting into the grounds. I've got my badge too, and I'll be sitting in the back of the car."

"Thanks, Peter. Do we show the badges to someone or put them through a card reader?"

"We hand them over to the guard on duty at the main gate, and he'll be the one to scan them. You don't need to worry, it'll all go fine. This isn't the first time I've done this sort of thing."

William turned to John saying that he wanted to speak to him alone for a moment. His friend was surprised by the request, but nodded, asking Peter to give them a minute. John got out of the car and he and William walked a few feet away.

"John, I don't trust this guy!"

"Why not? He's one of us, and he's giving us our only chance to get into Minedal-e!"

"The thing is he's not telling the truth! When someone lies, their words and actions tend to go out of sync, or rather the hand and arm movements are not synchronized with the words and seem mechanical, almost disconnected with the speech. That's what Peter's doing! A truthful person tends to move his limbs in synchrony to lend more emphasis to his thoughts."

"Listen, Will, you specialized in psychology and seem very attentive to body language, but please trust me and Peter."

"All right, I might be wrong. Let's go back to Peter."

They went back to join Peter, who had got out of the car and, visibly irritated, asked John, "Everything OK?"

"Yeah, everything's fine, go ahead and tell us the plan."

"All right. So once we've got the car into the grounds of the pharmaceutical company, we'll head for building number one. It's easy to recognize because it has huge colored glass windows you can see from the outside. Near the main entrance, low down, hidden behind a hedge, there is an electrical panel with the door open. We only need to lower the switch inside to cut off the power in the building. The first thing the secretary at reception will do is go and check the electrical panel in a room off the entrance hall. The surveillance video cameras will be deactivated, and then we'll have about fifteen minutes before the workers realize what has actually happened and turn the power back on. Once we are inside, we'll go to Shelton Malthen's office. Don't worry about him because he's out of town for a conference."

"It seems like the perfect plan. Did you set it up yourself?" asked William in a sarcastic tone.

"Of course, I planned it with some other members of the resistance. If you don't believe me, I can introduce you to them."

The tension was rapidly rising.

"Do you work for Shelton Malthen?" asked William, blatantly provocative.

An expression of surprise appeared on Peter's face because he wasn't expecting that question, and then he replied, "No, I do not work for Shelton Malthen."

William turned to John, unconcerned that Peter could hear. "Let me explain something to you. When a person lies, he tends to give negative answers using the same words that the questioner used because it's easier to repeat what he said than to risk giving himself away with needless details. So to the question, 'Do you work for Shelton Malthen?' Peter replied, 'No, I do not work for Shelton Malthen.' He's lying!"

Peter took on an angry expression, scratched his cheek, and then exclaimed, "John, your friend is accusing me! Do you want my help or not?"

William didn't even give John the time to answer. "You see, John? Did you notice the gestural slip? He scratched his cheek with his middle finger. That is a telltale sign and an emblem. It shows what Peter would like to say but doesn't. Do you know the meaning of the raised middle finger in certain past cultures? What's more, look at him, he has his chest facing towards us, but his feet and legs are pointed the other way, which means he wants to get away from here because he's been exposed. Do you need any more proof?"

"William, what are you saying?"

"John, let's just the two of us go to Minedal-e. If I'm wrong, when it's all over, I'll apologize to you both. Unless we do as I say, I'll find another way of getting into that building to rescue Beatrice."

John shook his head and apologized to Peter, asking him to understand his friend's emotional state. "William has lost his career and he actually doesn't have a life anymore. He's seen lots of people die around him and the woman he loves is being held hostage. Please try to understand."

Peter opened his arms wide in a sign of resignation. "I'm finding it hard to understand, but anyway the jumpsuits are in the back and so are the badges. I'll call a taxi and get out of your way. Anyway, if I had helped you, I might have lost my job and even my life. Much better this way. Good luck!"

5. Checkmate

John opened the door of his car and waited for William to get in, and they set off together for the pharmaceutical company's headquarters. On the way, neither said a word. The Peter episode had clearly created tension between them. Before reaching their destination, John pulled up to the side of the road so that they could put on the workman's jumpsuits, and William took the chance to apologize to John, saying that he had overdone it by acting as he did to Peter. While accepting his apology, John was still visibly annoyed.

They got to Minedal-e Corporation and greeted the security guard on the main gate, handing over their badges. John's was accepted with no problem, and the little light on the card reader flashing green, but William's didn't seem to work. Without taking his eyes off them as they sat in the car, the guard made a telephone call. The minutes passed and the tension increased.

"Maybe he has already realized that the badge was counterfeit, and he's calling for backup," thought William, gripping his pistol in his right hand.

The guard came back, and turning to John, said that his badge was in order, then he explained that the other had gotten demagnetized, and they could request a duplicate at the personnel office. The gate opened, and the car entered the grounds of Minedal-e Corporation. William knew the route to take to reach building number one because he had met Shelton Malthen there the time before. At the building they parked the car and, just as Peter had said, they found the electrical panel with the door open. At this point William thought he might have been wrong about Peter; if he had wanted to betray them in all probability the Minedal-e operatives would have already killed them. Once they had turned off the power in the building, as expected, the secretary got up and left her workstation. They walked immediately in through the main entrance and quickly reached the double wooden doors to Shelton Malthen's office. Beatrice can't have been far, William's heart was in his mouth, and right then all he wanted to do was to hold her again and then take her somewhere safe to begin a new life.

No sooner had they opened the door than something incredible and totally unexpected occurred: Dr. David Shelton Malthen was sitting at his desk and next to him, tied to a chair and clearly unconscious, was Beatrice. Not far away, Peter was sitting comfortably in an armchair reading a magazine. David was wearing a very elegant dark blue velvet suit, his hair was brushed back, and he was looking at them with a deep, penetrating stare. At first, he didn't say a word, but he didn't seem at all surprised to see William in his office, then he spoke. "Come on Mr. Pattern, John please show him in."

John pointed his pistol at William's back and then rapidly removed both his pistols, saying, "Sorry, but you're paying for your stubbornness!"

William felt a stabbing pain around his heart. He couldn't believe that his best friend had betrayed him. "No, it couldn't be true, it must be a nightmare," he thought.

Unfortunately, nightmares are sometimes real and there is no way you can make them disappear by waking up. David said sarcastically, "So, Mr. Pattern, how is your passionate pursuit of the truth coming along?"

William lunged forward to try to hit David, but John held him back by his arm. Then, with studied indifference, David said, "I wouldn't do that if I were you, because John might shoot your sweetheart and ruin her pretty face. That really would be a great ending: your best friend killing the love of your life! Don't tempt me, William! Your adventure ends here and soon you will be keeping your father company in the afterlife. First, however, allow me to thank you for enabling us to eliminate the resistance almost completely. I am a reasonable person and above all a merciful one, so before killing you and your wife, I will give you one more emotional thrill by telling you how I saved the world."

After a brief pause, with a touch of pride and the air of one who is about to solve a mystery, David continued with his story. "Hydrosolubility! With this great discovery, I paid tribute to the memory of my father! If he could only see what I have succeeded in creating from his research, he would be very proud of me and my team of scientists. My father was an idealist and really wanted to save humanity, so he set to work and found the vaccine to defeat the terrible virus that threatened to destroy the human race. But soon he realized that humanity would become extinct anyway if it continued to be slave to emotions, and so he developed Em 0."

"So depriving everyone of their emotions? Criminal!"

"Let me finish. For some strange, reason there were people who showed some resistance to Em 0, but it would have been impossible to inject everyone with a second dose. By mixing Em 0 with various substances, forgive me if I don't go into detail by listing them all, as not being an expert you wouldn't understand, we managed to create a hydrosoluble serum. When a schoolteacher, for instance, informed us of a child who appeared to show emotions, we intervened by simply making the child drink a glass of water in which Em 0 was dissolved. In our great magnanimity, we gave everyone a second chance to redeem themselves. Then if the second dose of the serum did not have an effect, we proceeded with the physical elimination of the subject."

"You are a ruthless criminal. You show no compassion, even for children!" cried William.

"It is the inevitable price to pay for a better society!" said Peter cynically, breaking into the conversation.

David did not like to be interrupted and wanted to keep control of the conversation, so he made a hand gesture at Peter intimating that he should remain silent, and went on, "We became aware that a second dose of the serum acted with greater strength on some memories, partially canceling them. So, just for the record, although you certainly won't remember any of this, Beatrice really is your wife, and you used to live together. But you were going a step too far with your emotions and you were becoming dangerous to MC. You will forgive the expression, but you have both acted as guinea pigs for our experiments and now I'll explain why."

"Guinea pigs?"

"Precisely. Among the researchers on my team, there were those who maintained that two doses of Em 0 were too little to completely remove the emotions and memories of the more refractory subjects. So, over time, we administered both you and your wife with several doses of Em 0, and yet neither emotions nor memories were completely wiped out. You should be pleased to have helped scientific research, albeit unwittingly. Today, thanks to your contribution, we have further confirmation of what we imagined. So, if after receiving a second dose of Em 0, a person continues to have memories or feel even toned-down emotions, we do not administer a third or fourth dose but kill them immediately."

"Respect for life has no value for you, and to think that millions of people admire you, if they only knew…" William didn't get to the end of his sentence because David, disregarding him completely, continued to speak, raising his voice. "Your father Virgilio was one of the most brilliant minds at Minedal-e Corporation. I would say he had true talent, until one day he decided to rebel, and not only did he steal our secrets, but he also founded the criminal organization that goes by the name of Emosemvi. We had spies everywhere and through our collaboration with Chief of Police McMillan we discovered what the resistance was plotting. We started to hunt it down until we identified a building in Calicraston Ville as one of their branches, and we were lucky because Virgilio was actually there at the time. That day I put an end to his worthless life, burying his dreams of glory and his emotions right there in that building."

Clenching his fists, William was attempting to control his growing anger. He wanted to avoid having his judgment clouded at such a critical moment when he needed to stay lucid and rational. Still, he couldn't help himself from muttering between his teeth, "You'll pay for this."

David pointed his finger at him, exclaiming, "But, the true key player is you! Without you, it wouldn't have been possible to put an end to your father's dream. In a way, we're similar you and I, don't you think? We both want to pay tribute to our father by continuing his work."

"I'll never be like you!"

"You're so naive! Let me add one last detail. We got our hands on Reversing, and John injected himself with it just to make you believe that he was a "free" man. That let him to infiltrate the resistance too. You were together when we tried to have you run over by a car, remember? Everything was supposed to end that day, but our assassin didn't succeed in killing you, and you ended up in the hospital. So we changed our plans and we let you live with the sole aim of destroying the resistance. I should thank you for helping us nearly get rid of it altogether. That evening at the garage..."

David turned to John, asking, "What was it called again?"

"Gear Jesture, sir."

"Oh, yes! At Gear Jesture John wore a bright red hat. You remember that, don't you? It was a sign to distinguish him from everyone else in the smoky garage and our operatives were briefed not to shoot him. That evening you were meant to die, but you made it through once again, so we had to lure you here to kill you. We even gave Peter a shot of Reversing to make it all the more credible, but it seems that you've got quite good at sniffing out lies. In a way, I admire your talent! We could have killed you at any point, but I'm a sentimental man, and I wanted to end this story right here, in the very place that your father Virgilio began his criminal career."

Any chance of escape was dwindling as the minutes passed, and now the game with destiny seemed as good as lost. The echo of David's last words was still in the air when for a brief instant Beatrice opened her eyes, and that was enough to reawaken a feeble hope in William's heart. He admitted, "I know when I'm beat. But before I die at least tell me how I saw my mother in the video of a wedding with Dr. Paul Shelton Malthen. Did they know each other?"

"Your mother worked here, and she was very gifted."

"Where are you keeping her prisoner?"

"Prisoner?" asked David sneering. "As you can imagine, there is no love lost between your mother and me." Then after a short pause, he added, "I know nothing about her."

Slowly William started to walk back and forth, then he said, "One last thing. Do you know what emblems are?"

David did not answer the question, and the room fell into a deep silence. "Of course, you don't! Emblems are those intentional or unintentional movements that substitute words. When I asked you where my mother was held prisoner, you held the index finger of your right hand in front of your nose. This is the emblem of silence. It is used when someone intends to say something but is inhibited by the presence of another person or talking about a particular subject. So you know many things about my mother that you do not intend to say."

"I congratulate you, but now the time for games is over! John, kill him quickly and take care not to get blood on the carpet."

While William was talking to David, he was intentionally walking back and forth to get closer to John so that, when the time came, he could turn and disarm him. But things did not go quite like that. William turned suddenly, but he didn't manage to disarm John who fired a bullet that lodged in the ceiling. In the ensuing scuffle, John punched William in the face and then kneed him repeatedly in the stomach. Meanwhile, David took a pistol out of a drawer, but he didn't fire it because as the two of them were struggling with each other, he risked hitting the wrong man. John fired another three bullets himself and one of them scratched the palm of William's left hand, making him cry out in pain. David decided to shoot because now his life was in danger and he no longer cared whether he hit John. And that is exactly what happened, the gunshot from the pistol hit John straight in the back. William could then grab his pistol and return fire, hitting David in the chest and Peter in the left leg.

David was lying on the floor and William went up to him. "I know where my mother is, and I will rescue her. This is where the dream of the Shelton Malthens comes to its end!"

David was having trouble breathing and his dark blue velvet suit was stained in blood. "Your mother has only ever caused trouble. I am just a pawn, a small tile in a bigger mosaic. Good and evil have always been in balance, and we are the good…"

He didn't finish his sentence because his heart stopped beating.

Peter was lying on the floor moaning in pain, and William pointed his pistol at him meaning to shoot him. They looked each other in the eye for a moment, then William lowered the pistol, deciding to spare his life. He felt pity for the man, even though he was a traitor. Peter's eyes showed a deep sadness, and William wanted to give him the chance to go on experiencing that for the rest of his life.

In the meantime, Beatrice had opened her eyes, but she was clearly in a semi-conscious state. They might have sedated her. William untied her hands and asked her if she could walk, but she didn't answer. She looked very weak and a bloodstain on her white blouse was getting larger. One of the shots fired during the fight had hit her in the stomach. William didn't have time to staunch the wound, so he took her in his arms, grabbed his pistols, and headed down the corridor with the large colored glass windows framed in lead to the exit.

5.1

From the reception at the end of the corridor, the security men's voices could be heard. The secretary had probably alerted security when she heard the shots. William eased Beatrice down onto the floor so that his hands were free to break one of the large glass windows with the butt of his pistol. The glass shattered and made an alternative exit. With Beatrice in his arms, William walked around the building, in front of which four security vehicles were parked with their doors still open, but empty inside. It was the time to act. He put Beatrice on the back seat of one of the cars then he used the two-way radio to call the guard on the main gate of Minedal-e, telling him to open the gate because a vehicle would be leaving immediately on urgent business.

He sped the security car, hurtling through the main gate of the pharmaceutical company, and after a few miles, he noticed in the rearview mirror that the other Minedal-e vehicles were following him. In an attempt to shake them off, he accelerated until the car was at full speed and he got to the highway where the traffic seemed heavy. He drove as fast as possible along the shoulder until after a few miles he turned off down a dusty country road. Meanwhile, his pursuers had gained ground and were on his heels. Reaching a state road he could increase speed in the hopes of losing them, but one of them bumped his car, then came alongside him and tried to force him off the road. William was faster and swerved rapidly banging into the security car and making it veer into a guardrail. By this time Beatrice had regained consciousness and started to moan in pain. She was losing a lot of blood and the gunshot wound was painful.

"Sweetheart, try to press down on the wound with your hand. We're almost there!" cried William.

"Where are we?"

"It's a long story, but try to keep your eyes open and talk to me, OK?"

Without answering Beatrice collapsed on the back seat again, losing consciousness. "Damn it!" thought William, as he wrapped a white bandage found in the glove compartment around his left hand. The security cars were still on his tail, one of them came up next to him and tried to force him off the road. William took out his pistol and shot at the car's front wheel sending it crashing into the iron pole of a road sign. Beatrice didn't utter a word and had stopped moaning, and it wasn't clear now whether she was dead or just unconscious. With one last Minedal-e car still chasing them, though a ways off, they reached Anger City airport and pulled into the parking lot. William abandoned the car from the pharmaceutical company and moved Beatrice into the back seat of his own car and then he off for the Anger City hospital where he soon arrived.

At the sight of the wounded woman, the nurses ran over to take her and then placed her on a stretcher. William knew he couldn't stay there because if anyone had recognized him, they would inform the men from Minedal-e Corporation. Luckily, although Beatrice was unconscious, her heart was still beating. William kissed her, squeezed her hand, and, just as he was about to leave, he unclasped the necklace with the heart-shaped pendant, saying, "I'll give it back to you as soon as you're better. Together, beyond the bounds of emotions. I love you." The world around them seemed to stop for an instant as though it wanted to give the young lovers the chance to say goodbye, possibly for the last time. Stowed away in their hearts was the hope of living a future together, and in their souls, the desire to love each other forever.

CHAPTER THREE:

The Earth's Belly

1. An unexpected journey

William went back to his car, took off the workman's jumpsuit and changed into the clothes he had in his bag. Then he drove into downtown Happiness City and took the elevator up to the top floor of the skyscraper where his grandfather used to take him as a kid. He needed to think and just then he had no idea where to go.

It is in this very place that our story began:

William's hand was wrapped in a white, blood-stained bandage and in it, he held a necklace with heart-shaped pendant with the letter "W" engraved in the center. The words he spoke were lost in the air, "Together, beyond the bounds of emotions."

Soon he would be arrested and sentenced to death; the sound of police sirens was disappearing into the leaden sky but would soon grow louder until the police were surrounding the skyscraper. A tear ran down his face, blending with the raindrops as if the sky were moved to compassion by the intensity of William's sadness and wanted to be part of his weeping.

The Minedal-e operatives had alerted their police infiltrators, and William was now on borrowed time; they knew where he was and would soon be on him. He decided to make one last phone call from his cell phone to Leonardo, after all he was the only person left alive whom he could still trust. "Leo!"

"William! Where have you been? You've been accused of murder, your picture is all over the news, and the police even suspect me!"

"I haven't got much time to explain what happened. Minedal-e Corporation controls the police, and even Chief of Police McMillan is corrupt."

"First, how are you?" asked Leonardo.

"My hand was grazed by a bullet, but I'm OK."

"Tell me where you are. I'll come and get you."

"It's too late, in less than a week, my world has fallen apart. I want to go and rescue my mother. She's being held in a secret location in Niger that belongs to Minedal-e Corporation."

"Let me help you. Tell me where you are, Will!"

"I've already dragged you into this thing far enough, and I don't want to risk your life. These people don't play around, and you'd end up in a plastic bag in a couple of hours. I'm touched you want to help me. You're a real friend. Maybe someday, we can be friends in an easy, fun way, and even laugh like crazy and get carried away like they were in the old world. You should try emotions, my friend. They're fantastic! Now I have to go. Goodbye."

Leonardo didn't have time to answer because William abruptly ended the conversation, turning off his cell phone and putting it back in his pocket. He suddenly thought of Romance, the man in the coat with the fur collar he met the evening of the ambush at Gear Jesture. He could get him to Niger without going through customs, after all he worked in import-export at the port in Contempt City and, if they hadn't already caught him, he really might be the only person who could help. William was devastated by everything that had happened to him recently, but he still clung to the faint hope of embracing his mother and Beatrice again.

He took the elevator down to the garage where he had parked the car and drove away at full speed because soon the police would be closing the surrounding streets.

William reached Contempt City port, where unlike Happiness City the sky was clear, and the sun warmed the earth, stroking the white cliffs with its rays, and seagulls spun in the sky giving the scene a sense of peace and freedom. The only entrance to the port was guarded by the personnel of a private security firm that checked every vehicle had the authorization to enter.

He parked the car by the side of the street and sat on a wall for a while to watch the traffic that went in and out of the port, and then he saw his chance and he certainly wasn't going to let it go. A truck belonging to Romance's company, Rotaon Ltd, was approaching the entrance to the port. He jumped down from the wall and ran along the side of the street, and just as the truck passed, he launched himself into the truck bed, which was covered by a thick plastic sheet. The truck got to the entrance to the port, the guards waved it through without conducting any kind of inspection and when it came to a stop, William waited a moment before getting out. Once out of the truck, he looked around him; there were lots of metal containers on the dock and as many again in an area not far away, facing him was a tall building with wooden walls and a large sign saying Rotaon Ltd. The sign looked the worse for wear, and beneath the peeling green paint you could see traces of the old red paint showing through.

His ex-colleague John had been at Gear Jesture the night of the resistance meeting and would certainly have informed the men from Minedal-e of the role Romance played in Emosemvi. There was no doubt Romance was in danger and who could say if he were still alive. He went through a wooden door into the company's management offices, in front of him a middle-aged woman with curly hair tied back sat behind a desk consulting a large maritime register. She was probably Romance's secretary, but he had to proceed carefully because he was not sure whether she worked for Rotaon Ltd or was an undercover operative for Minedal-e Corporation. The woman greeted him cordially. "What can I do for you?"

"My name is William, and I'm looking for someone."

"I'm Maggie and I might be able to help you."

"Does Romance work here?"

"No, I've never heard the name."

"I talked to him a while ago, and he said he worked here."

"No, I'm afraid I can't help you," said the woman turning towards her computer screen to end the conversation.

"Are you sure? Because I noticed that you made incongruous movements."

Sorry, what did you say?" Maggie clearly felt uncomfortable, she didn't like a stranger asking her so many questions and was becoming suspicious.

"When I asked you if Romance worked here, you replied no but for a fraction of a second you nodded your head. So your nonverbal language contradicted you. Basically, you lied in what you said, but you didn't succeed in doing the same with your body. Now, please, would you tell me where my friend is?"

"I don't know what you are talking about," answered Maggie, annoyed and making it clear that her patience was coming to an end.

"The only question is whether you are lying to protect my friend or whether you work for the pharmaceutical company," went on William undeterred, going up to the desk.

"That's enough! I'm calling security!"

Just as Maggie picked up the telephone to call the port security guards, a door opened behind her and Romance appeared. "It's all right Maggie, I know this man. Follow me, William."

The two men disappeared through the door into a large room with an old wooden desk surrounded by cardboard boxes scattered around the floor. On the desk sat a small marble statue of a mythological hero holding a spear. Romance pushed it forward and a secret trapdoor opened in the floor. They went down some steps into an underground room hidden beneath the trapdoor where there was an old bed with a mattress covered in mold and not far away dozens of submachine guns in a pile, explosives, large amounts of ammunition and about forty vials of Reversing.

Romance said, "Maggie is always very careful. Please forgive her. She takes a major risk coming here, More than once, I've told her she should go and work in her husband's restaurant in Anger City, but she's always refused. She's a stubborn Irish woman!"

"No problem, I completely understand. She's right to be careful and her sense of duty is admirable."

"This is the last bastion of the resistance. There aren't many of us left and there is no one who can go against Shelton Malthen. I took refuge here, but they're looking for me. They haven't caught me yet because the port is protected by an international agreement, so neither Minedal-e Corporation nor the police have jurisdiction here. But that won't stop our enemies from storming it. Reversing is not easy to find, and those you see there are among the only vials left in the world," said Romance as he picked up some bullets that had fallen out of an ammunition case.

"David Shelton Malthen is dead, and my ex colleague from the police was a spy, but he's not a problem anymore either," revealed William in a solemn voice.

Romance opened his eyes wide, going over to William and hugging him. "Really? That criminal doctor got what he deserved for all the deaths he caused. And I had my doubts about your colleague from the start. What was his name... Oh yeah, now I remember, John! That night at Gear Jesture old Tobias died, as did all the other members of the resistance. The men from MC left their dead bodies at the garage for several hours, thinking they would catch us as soon as we went back to get them in order to give them a decent burial. They laid a trap for us, but we didn't fall for it."

"I'm sorry about Tobias and the others. They were good people. We must continue our fight and avenge them. I need to get to Africa. Do you think you can help me?"

"To Africa, William? We need to focus our efforts here and now, not somewhere else!"

"I know, but I have to go to Africa. I need to get to MC's secret location. My mother is being held there."

"I see. The time has come for me to tell you a secret. A while ago one of our spies came back from Africa. In his report he said there was an underground bunker called Tartarus where thousands of vials of EM 0 are produced to be sent to countries in the east. The spy who came back from Africa was named George, and he was the owner of Marleyes restaurant in Surprise City. You've met Stan, his son. For security reasons George kept the first half of the coordinates to reach the MC bunker and then gave the other half to his brother Tim, an eccentric guy with a scruffy beard and long white hair. The coordinates don't only show the whereabouts of the bunker, but also contain a secret message, though no one has ever been able to decipher it."

William opened his eyes wide. He couldn't believe what he was hearing. "Incredible! The mystery intensified. What is the code hidden within the coordinates?" he thought.

Romance added, "George also discovered something else. It seems unbelievable, but MC's real HQ is there in Africa, and David Shelton Malthen was only a puppet with someone else pulling the strings. George found out the identity of this despicable puppet master, but he didn't manage to tell anyone before he was killed."

"Poor George, he took the secret to his grave. Who knows if we will ever find out who is hiding behind MC."

"I can tell you right now, Will. Paul Shelton Malthen had two sons, David and Ross. The brothers were always very competitive; both wanted the attention of their father, who, nevertheless, showed more respect for Ross. But one day Ross disappeared, and no one ever found out what had happened to him. Some believe that he died in a car accident, but in all likelihood, Ross is in Africa in Tartarus the bunker, and he is the leader of MC. Before he died, old Paul strategically divided the world into two, the east and the west, and then he entrusted their government to his two sons, naming Ross his sole heir. In this way, the Shelton Malthen brothers got the two things most desired by people of the old world: power and money."

"I met George at the Marleyes before he died, and I met his brother Tim at the police station where he use to work undercover. I have the coordinates and the bunker is located in the desert of Niger. But I didn't find a secret message in the coordinates."

"Ah! That's why you mentioned Niger. That changes everything! It doesn't surprise me that your mother is being held prisoner there because she worked with your father on a secret project in the laboratories at MC. Many employees were forced to work for Shelton Malthen even against their will. Some of them mysteriously disappeared. At first, we thought they'd been killed, but their skills were useful to MC, so they kidnapped them and made them work in the secret laboratories."

Romance was the only person who could help him, and he desperately hoped that he could find a way to get him to Africa.

"OK, can I count on your help?" asked William, full of hope.

"Yes, tomorrow you can board one of my ships bound for the port of Dakar in Senegal. Then to reach Niger you'll have to cross Mali and Burkina Faso too. The journey will be full of hidden dangers, and you'll have to fight to get across those desolate lands so you can stock up with weapons here. If you wear my transport company's green jumpsuit no one will ask questions at the port in Dakar, and there you must go to the management office and ask for Castor. He'll help you with your journey. I've got no way of contacting him to notify him of your arrival. My phone is certainly under surveillance and the call would be intercepted, but I don't think you'll have a problem identifying yourself as a member of the resistance because you know our code."

"It's all clear."

"I really don't know what you'll find in that bunker, but if you blow it up, you'd give the resistance a hope of victory. And if you managed to get rid of Ross, humanity would be in your debt."

"OK Romance, thanks, I'm ready to leave. One more thing. My wife Beatrice Whites is in the Anger City hospital with a gunshot wound. I'd be grateful if you could keep her safe from the MC operatives. They might already know where she is and will try to kill her."

"Don't worry, I'll find a way of protecting her."

"Thanks, I really appreciate it."

That night, William only managed to sleep a couple of hours because the secret hideaway full of weapons and ammunition had a strong smell of mold.

1.1

The following morning he put two semi-automatic guns, some ammunition, a GPS device and five vials of Reversing in a bag. Romance brought him fruit for breakfast, then he handed him the green Rotaon Ltd jumpsuit and accompanied him to the quay of a large ship packed tight with containers on the main deck.

The resistance was on the verge of being beaten, the chances of victory seemed remote, and, in a way, William was the only person who could strike down Minedal-e Corporation. They hugged each other and said goodbye, and in their eyes was the shadow of hope that they might meet again, but neither knew if that could really happen. William's journey might only be one way, but he didn't fear death, as his heart was full of love for Beatrice and there was no room for any other feeling.

The great ship he was to board was docked at quay eighteen; on its side was the image of a terracotta vase bearing the name "Elpis." Lying on top of it, like great sleeping titans, were several large colored containers and when the ship set sail their slumber was obviously disturbed because they stirred slightly.

William was not traveling in a cabin like the other sailors, but in the hold, where he made space for himself by some wooden packing cases with the wood-burned brand of the shipping company "Astoria 1985" on them. He only went on deck to get to the canteen and quickly eat something. He had no intention of becoming friendly with the other members of the crew, in fact, he could trust no one. Among them were some colorful characters such as the cook Jack, bald with a thick black beard, whose angular face made one think of the hard lines of sea cliffs. Then there was a sailor with an attentive expression named Mikey and a tall, fat man with short hair and a wayward cowlick by the name of Clark. The ship's captain was named Willy. He seemed to have come straight out of a pirate book, he wore a patch over his left eye and had a very unreassuring appearance, but the crew respected him and carried out his orders to the letter.

The journey to Dakar took several days, and right in the middle of the ocean the ship was hit by a violent storm, and to avoid being thrown into the air, William had to tie himself to a metal bar. Fortunately, the storm passed, the sky opened, and the sun sent its rays over the ocean's water, which with its gurgling spume seemed to sing a hymn to the beauty of nature.

William spent the days reading old sailing manuals that he found in the hold, simulating facial expressions in front of a mirror and letting his thoughts go to Beatrice in her hospital bed. He also stopped to reflect on the importance of thought and the emotions. "Thinking of someone far away makes their absence less hard to bear, and at the same time, it is also the best way to exercise the right of freedom belonging to every human being. Even with chains on your wrists you can think, and no one can stop you, and when memories fill the mind inevitably the emotions are sparked. They obey no master and thumb their notice of every tool of coercion."

Finally, after several days, the ship docked at sunset at the wharf in Dakar, William saw the light of the sun again and at the same time he noticed how much more like an open-air market the port was, full of street vendors. There you could buy any type of merchandise, from craftwork and food to contraband goods and even weapons. The street vendors' faces lacked expression, obviously MC and its Em 0 had gotten there too, as they had every remote corner of the planet.

Before disembarking, William put on the Rotaon Ltd green jumpsuit, then he slung the bag over his shoulder and headed for the management office. On his way he was stopped several times by people wanting to sell him things, had he more time and money he would certainly have helped the local economy by buying something, but it was late, and darkness was gradually pushing the sun down into the sea. At that latitude, the sun seemed larger than the other parts of the world, and William watched it as it sank into the ocean, tingeing the sky and sea with its fiery light.

Many street vendors were chewing little pieces of wood, presumably a local custom; their faces were expressionless, and yet you could make out the typical traits of the dignity of people who struggle to survive in a world with few opportunities.

William reached the port's sole building, a two-floor construction of clay bricks and wide metal bands. Inside, in a large room, many sailors were in a line to hand in transport documents to the customs officials. Judging by the number of people in the office it would take hours for the line to dwindle. William went up to an official to ask where he could find his contact, but he was bluntly told to go and get in line with the others, or else he might get attacked by the crowd. Getting the message, he went and sat on a wooden bench to wait to talk to someone.

Just past midnight the large room had emptied of people, only the cleaning staff and management clerks remained; an old woman with white hair and dark eyes by the name of Leda went up to William asking if he worked for Rotaon Ltd. At that moment her son Castor joined them, and after thanking his mother, he asked, "Who sent you here?"

"Romance sent me. I'm happy to meet you. My name is William," he said in a low voice and using the resistance code, hoping that he was talking with a member of Emosemvi.

"I am not happy, and I don't know anyone called Romance, sir."

"I've probably got the wrong person. I shouldn't have asked for you. I need to find somewhere to spend the night. I don't think it's safe here and it frightens me," added William, showing the emotions of contempt and then fear.

With an expression of anger, Castor answered, "You have to look elsewhere. I advise you to leave."

"I'm sorry that you can't help me," said William with a sad expression.

"I'm Castor. Follow me, there's not much time!"

Castor had correctly interpreted the resistance code and went over to a utility room full of brooms and cleaning products, closing the door behind them. "How are things with Romance?"

"Not good. Unfortunately the police are looking for him and the resistance has nearly been wiped out completely. Do you know if there is an MC base in Niger?"

"No, I don't know anything about that. Do you need to get to Niger?"

"Yes, and quickly."

"You've no idea, William, what I would do to smash MC and its operatives. Those bastards killed my brother a while back. He was a boxer and had been training in the gym when he was surrounded by five men. After interrogating him to see if he belonged to the resistance, they beat him up and though he fought like a lion, he died fighting. I dream of a better world where criminals like them are punished. All I have left in the world are my mother and my son Michael, who is a policeman and works at Happiness City police station. For some reason, he has always refused to inject himself with Reversing."

"Yes, I know the police station at Happiness City, I worked there too and I'm truly sorry about your brother, unfortunately those killers show no mercy for anyone."

"Be at dock twenty-three at dawn tomorrow. Someone will pick you up in a truck. It'll be easy to recognize him because he'll be carrying sheep and the truck will have a white shell with a cross on top painted on the sides. Your journey won't be easy and there's a fair chance you won't get there alive because you'll be traveling over land controlled by the men from MC. I'm offering my help, but I need something in return."

"What is it, Castor?"

"I need guns and some vials of Reversing. Things aren't good here. This country is devastated by poverty. We are not technologically advanced like other nations because MC chose Africa as the first place in the world to spread Em 0. Along with emotions, the chance of progressing from a social point of view here also disappeared, and unfortunately they've deprived us of everything."

"That's terrible. Let's hope we manage to beat MC, otherwise there is no future for this country and for the world."

"The need to live in a better place keeps us going," said Castor emphatically.

"I agree with you. About the guns, can't you buy them from one of the street vendors?"

"Are you kidding, William? MC operatives are everywhere, and I can't risk getting caught. If I bought a weapon, they'd be onto me within the hour."

"OK, then take my bag. Everything you need is inside. Just let me keep the GPS and my clothes. I don't need any more guns because I must travel light, and I've still got my pistol and my Second Chance."

"Second chance?"

"Yeah, it's a long story. There's almost no one I can trust in the world, but a friend named Leonardo suggested years ago that I keep a second pistol at my ankle. You never know what may happen when bullets start flying."

Castor thanked him for the bag containing the gear he needed, and then as they said goodbye, he hugged him and wished him good luck.

William went back to the ship, where he slept for a few hours. It was interesting to see how by day the cries of the street vendors echoed among the containers in the port smothering every other noise, but by night it was the lapping of the sea that filled the air. In this place, the stars seemed brighter, as if their shining was inspired by an intense compassion for the people of these lands.

2. Jungle of emotions

At dawn William changed out of the green jumpsuit into his own clothes, then he made his way to dock twenty-three, but there was no one waiting for him. Just then he realized that he had left his coat on the ship, but at that latitude it was very hot, and he definitely wouldn't need it. After a few hours, a truck with the painted symbol on its side of a white shell topped with a cross, finally turned up and stopped in front of him. A tall, thin man got out, with eyes dark as pitch, wearing a mechanic's overalls stained with grease. After looking around him warily, the man, who was carrying a strange musical instrument with strings, turned to him saying, "Are you William? My name is Orpheus, and I suppose you need a ride to Niger."

Orpheus flashed an expression of happiness, William gave him a smile saying, "Yes, that's me, and I'd be happy to travel with you."

"Sorry to disappoint you, but you'll be traveling in the back with the sheep. The smell is disgusting but after a while

197

you'll get used to it. It's a long way and will take us several days," said Orpheus, expressing disgust.

"OK, no problem, I'm not worried."

The two men swapped a conspiratorial look as their brief exchange was enough to identify each other as members of Emosemvi. Orpheus got into the driver's seat of the truck while William climbed into the back where the sheep took up the floor space, and in the corner, there was a pile of fodder. The black tarp that covered the cargo bed had metal eyelets along its edge through which William could peek, so he could find landmarks and recognize his way home if anything went wrong. African roads were rarely paved, and the dust swirled under the cover making the air almost unbreathable.

They traveled all day and finally in the evening Orpheus stopped near a forest, lit a fire and offered some tinned meat to his traveling companion, who was completely covered in dust and famished. The sky, full of stars, seemed even brighter than the night before and if there had still been one of those immortal ancient poets capable of stirring buried heart strings with words, he would certainly have put it to good use and composed his finest literary masterpiece.

Orpheus began to pluck the strings of the strange musical instrument, used in ancient times, called a "lyre." He talked about his wife and how the men from MC had taken her prisoner. She was a scientist and was working on a very important project, but precisely because she was so brilliant, she had been forced to work for the pharmaceutical company. After freeing her, the resistance offered her the chance to inject herself with Reversing, but she refused because once she had seen her husband cry and had been so shocked that she had ended up hating sadness.

The story resonated with William because those ruthless thugs had also kidnapped Beatrice.

Using the GPS, William showed his friend the location of the bunker belonging to MC where they were heading, then to make it clearer, with a small stick he drew the state of Niger in the ground, pointing to the exact place.

Meanwhile, the night had grown darker and the fire had ceased to dance and light up the surrounding plant life with its warm light. William threw another piece of wood on the embers and started to talk with Orpheus of the importance that emotions had in the human process of communication, and how useful it was to know how to interpret nonverbal signs. "Understanding whether our conversation partner is lying or telling the truth could save our life, especially if we are faced with an MC operative."

"I agree, but how can you tell if a person is lying?" asked Orpheus, curious.

"There are several ways of telling if the person we're talking to is being truthful. For instance, body movements to look at during a conversation are self-adaptors, with which different parts of the body are scratched, massaged and grasped. Self-adaptors increase in intensity and number when a person is under stress or ill at ease and, therefore, they can be indicators of lying."

"So if the person I'm talking to scratches his nose, he's lying?"

"No, Orpheus, it's not as simple as that because you must always place each act of communication within a larger framework. It is the sum of several signs that tells us whether we are talking to liar or a truthful person."

"You know a lot, don't you? I'm no great expert at psychology. I like music, and since I was a boy, I've always played a musical instrument, I don't know if it can really be considered a talent. This lyre, for example, was left to me by my father; before he died, he told me that music is the most powerful instrument for peace in the world, and with it you can stop a war and change the fate of many people."

Orpheus began to play the lyre, and a melody came from the instrument that was so exquisite that it even quietened the noise of the animals in the nearby forest, as though the notes soothed their souls by offering them peace. Soon that melody put the world to sleep, cradling its dreams with the fragrance of life. The night covered everything with its silence.

2.1

A moment before dawn broke, while Orpheus was loading a bundle of dry wood onto the back of the truck, William opened his eyes. His friend had given him a handkerchief and some odd aviator's glasses to help him to survive the dust that would come into the truck's cargo bed on the journey.

They set off at rapid clip, crossing first the border of Mali, then that of Burkina Faso. The journey was exhausting, and the truck's cargo bed became scorching in the heat while water supplies were rapidly dwindling. In Burkina Faso, they were stopped at a police roadblock controlled by Minedal-e Corporation. Through the metal eyelets at the edge of the truck's black tarp, William could see a soldier with a gun on his shoulder approach Orpheus. The soldier seemed suspicious and came around to inspect the back of the truck with another soldier. One of them climbed onto the cargo bed, which gave off a very bad smell from the sheep. Not finding anything irregular, he got back down almost immediately and told Orpheus to be on his way. No sooner had the truck started moving than William emerged from under the pile of animal fodder. At that moment he was amazed he was still alive because he could hardly breathe underneath the fodder, and he took a deep sigh of relief.

The truck had been traveling along the roads of Niger for hours, when the engine broke down near a village not far from their final destination. A local mechanic said he would repair the truck in return for two sheep. Since there was no alternative to giving into his demand, Orpheus accepted.

The mechanic's name was Gordon, and he was tall with frizzy hair and wore a yellow shirt with no buttons down the front and a pair of ripped shorts. While he got on with repairing the truck's engine in his decrepit repair shop, which actually looked more like an out-of-town market, his grandfather sat there on a wooden seat. He had an enigmatic face with features that were very like a woman's. He was dressed in an orange tunic, his long white hair fell down to his shoulders, and he wore a bandage across both eyes. After listening to what the old man had to say, Orpheus translated his message, "This man is called Tiresias and speaks an ancient language that has now almost completely disappeared. He thinks you are the man in the prophecy, and he has been waiting for you for a long time."

"I really don't think so. He must be confusing me with someone else," said William shaking his head.

"The old man thinks that you have come to bring peace to this village and the world. The prophecy tells of a man without emotions who crushes the evil that plagues this land."

"I'm sorry to disappoint Tiresias, but I do feel emotions, and I don't think I am the savior of the world. What evil plagues this land?"

"According to Tiresias, armed men take away the young men of the village by force to a place not far from here to dig the earth. None of them has ever returned to the village, except his grandson, Gordon."

Although Gordon was busy repairing the engine, he had been listening to the conversation. "Don't mind my grandfather, unfortunately we don't have many people to talk with here, so he makes up strange stories."

William went up to Gordon and in a threatening tone, said, "Listen to me, not far from here there is an underground bunker belonging to Minedal-e Corporation. Is that where they take the young people of the village to work?"

"I know nothing, sorry. I'm just a mechanic, and I've never heard of an underground bunker. My grandfather Tiresias loves to tell wild stories."

"Maybe I wasn't being clear, Gordon. When a person is lying or simply omitting something, he tends to gesticulate less. A liar would probably keep his hands in his pockets or merely hold them still, just as you are right now. That happens because the brain is using most of its resources to invent a lie, so there is less space to manage body movements. To get to the point, you are lying. I have come from a long way away. I've had a hard journey to get here, and I'm racing against time."

William seized the collar of Gordon's shirt with both hands, shouting, "Tell me the truth or this will be the last engine you repair in your life!"

"OK, OK, all right! Once a month, the men from Minedal-e take away young men from the village by force and make them dig the earth. Years ago, MC built an underground bunker called Tartarus. Now it seems they want to build another nearby."

William let his hands drop, continuing to listen closely to what Gordon had to say because it appeared to be valuable information.

"One morning, before dawn, they came to take me away to dig. Then one day, as I was working, I forgot to empty my bucket of earth in the cart, and a guard from MC realized this and punished me by whipping my back. When the shift ended, instead of returning to the dormitory, I hid among the remnants of a wooden barrel, covering myself with trash bags. After a bit someone came to pick up the trash with a truck, and I ended up in his trailer with the trash. The strong acrid smell made me lose consciousness and when I came round, I found myself in a dump. I managed to find the road home and to hide here. Every month, when the MC men come to the village to take the young men, I hide in the repair shop inside a cavity in the wall."

"Slavery is a terrible thing, Gordon. Didn't any of you try to rebel?"

"No, because nobody feels emotions. There isn't a grain of anger in the hearts of the villagers. Thanks to an old friend, I managed to get hold of a vial of Reversing and inject myself with it. I know about Emosemvi, but I'm not part of it. My grandfather has never rebelled either, even after what they did to him. Here in the village people believe that he can predict the future and the men from MC, maybe to intimidate the people, turned up one morning and blinded him, intimating that he should stop his prophesying."

"I'm very sorry for Tiresias. When do the men from MC next come to get the young men?"

"As I said, they come once a month. Tomorrow at 5:00 a.m. they'll gather in the village square, then they go from house to house taking the young men away."

"OK, Gordon, I need two metal hooks, a cord and a mask with a small oxygen canister. Do you think you can get them for me?"

"No problem, I've got so much junk in the garage that it won't be hard to find two metal hooks and a cord. As for the mask and oxygen, I could ask the local doctor, who can be trusted."

William said goodbye to Gordon, thanking him heartedly, then using Orpheus as an interpreter, he wished Tiresias good luck. Evening fell and with it came the time to say goodbye because the next day William would travel on to the bunker on his own. He had never revealed the reason for his trip to Orpheus, who had also never asked him about it. They both believed in the resistance and helped other members of the organization without question; the sense of brotherhood united them like an invisible thread.

William returned to Gordon's workshop, where a plastic bag was ready for him containing the two metal hooks, the cord and a mask connected to a small oxygen canister.

That evening there was no clamor in the village streets, all the people were at home and knew what would happen the following day, and though they felt no sadness, their moods were more anxious than usual.

Before dawn William made his way to the village square and hiding behind a thick berry bush, he waited for the Minedal-e Corporation vehicles. Not long after, two high-powered cars drove up as well as an old green school bus with the paint peeling off. On all the doors of the vehicles was the symbol of a triangle enclosed in a circle, inside which were two crossed swords beneath the initials "M" and "C."

Five men dressed in black and fully armed got out of the vehicles and in random order made their way round the village homes. William waited until they were far enough away then he went up to the school bus and sneaked beneath it. He tied himself to the undercarriage with the hooks and cord, attempting to lift himself as far as possible from the ground, and then he put on the mask connected to the oxygen canister, which would let him breathe despite the dust raised by the school bus as they went along. If the school bus drove over a rock on the way it would, in all probability, kill him.

After about an hour, the men in black returned to the square, they made the young men they'd gathered dig the earth get onto the school bus and soon the convoy moved off. William was hit by a cloud of dust, he held tight to the cord to avoid falling to the ground, but after about fifteen minutes a warning light on the canister lit up, indicating that the oxygen was nearly finished; he was still covered in dust when a stone hit his head knocking him unconscious. He came round soon afterwards, the oxygen was now gone, and he was suffocating, so he tried to untie the cord to let himself drop to the ground, but he was stuck. Just as he was about to fall unconscious again from a lack of oxygen, the school bus stopped outside the entrance to the Minedal-e Corporation bunker.

3. Mask of smiles

A security guard walked around the school bus inspecting the undercarriage for possible explosives with a mirror on a long pole. Fortunately, William was right in the middle of the vehicle's undercarriage in a shadow, so he wasn't spotted. Once the security check was over, the convoy drove a short distance before disappearing into a large hangar that was perfectly camouflaged in the desert. The occupants of the vehicles walked away while the young men brought in the school bus were led single file into the desert.

William managed to undo the cord and dropped to the ground. His muscles were sore, and he needed a few minutes to regain the feeling in his body; he headed towards some oil barrels and hid behind them for a moment to take stock of the place, and then he found an elevator. On the wall was an explanatory map of the underground bunker's four levels. On the first lower level was the armory, the maintenance and ventilation plants, and on the second lower level were the sleeping quarters, the infirmary and the canteen. At the third lower level were the management and logistical offices and the laboratories where Em 0 was produced, and at the fourth and lowest level, were the detention cells. Madeline would certainly be being held prisoner there, but even though the doors to the elevator were open it only seemed to work with a special key, and without that, it wouldn't take William anywhere.

He looked for the escape hatch on the elevator ceiling, and just as two men in black were approaching, he managed to pull out the lynch pin and climbed through the hatch to the maintenance area where the steel cables and pulleys were located. The elevator moved and stopped at minus two, then after a short pause it went back up to level minus one, then down to minus three. William waited a few minutes and opened the hatch and dropped down into the elevator, he pulled out his pistol and, after checking around for guards, went down a long corridor to reach the emergency stairs and on down to level minus four. His heart was thumping, and adrenaline had flooded his whole body. He was afraid his life would end in that bunker. But for his mother he was willing to do this and more, go all the way to hell if he had to.

He ran downstairs, reaching a room full of video camera screens, but there was no sign of any security guards, so he went in and pushed a large red button to open the cell doors in the first corridor. The cells were all empty and his hopes of finding Madeline were vanishing like soap bubbles hit by a sudden rush of wind. At one point he stopped outside a cell and stared wide-eyed: a quite elderly woman with long white hair and dressed in a coat was staring back at him. He looked closer and through the lines of her face he recognized the features of his mother, Madeline. In a voice breaking with emotion, he exclaimed, "Mom!"

"William, is it really you?" answered the woman in a trembling voice.

They held each other in such a close embrace that they could hardly breathe, then they began to cry, their hearts beating in unison and breaking the silence of those cold cells. Madeline found the strength to speak, "I didn't think you'd manage to come all this way!"

"I wouldn't have bet on it either, but I've done it."

"You've grown, my son. You look like your father," said the woman smiling.

"We've got so many things to tell each other. You'll see, we'll make up for all the lost time. I imagine it hasn't been easy for you being forced to work for these tyrants."

Madeline was staring at her son with her large brown eyes, as he went on, "Do you know how we can get out of here?"

"I'm sorry, William."

"What do you mean, Mom? Aren't you happy to see me?"

Suddenly a man dressed in black and holding a pistol appeared at the cell's doorway. William didn't immediately recognize him, because he would never have expected to see him there, but looking more closely, he felt shivers run through him and a pang in his heart, "Leonardo!"

It was his friend and classmate from the academy, Leonardo. What was he doing there? Why was he pointing a pistol at him?

"It was inevitable, William. You had to be stopped somehow."

Leonardo took his pistol away and made him follow him to the elevator with his mother. William was dumbfounded and put up no resistance. He had a million questions to which he could see no answers; Madeline's face showed no emotion, she simply lowered her eyes and remained silent. The elevator took them up to level minus three, then they proceeded down a corridor and into a large meeting room dimly lit with a defective neon light that flashed on and off at regular intervals.

Leonardo sat next to Madeline and made a gesture with his pistol for William to sit down.

After a moment's silence, his mother sighed deeply. "William, I really don't know where to begin. Your eyes have the same stubbornness as your father Virgilio's, and I never would have wanted it to come to this."

"You are the leader of Minedal-e Corporation! You are the one they call Campe!" cried William.

All at once, as though a veil had suddenly fallen from his eyes, everything made sense. He remembered the text of the letter written by Jacqueline to Virgilio, "Minedal-e Corporation has spies everywhere. I hate the witch at the head of that organization. If I could, I would kill her with my own hands!" Virgilio too, in the video message he left for William at the Eversten movie theater, though almost too moved to speak, before being interrupted, said the following words, "One more thing, my boy. The time has come to talk about your mother. It gives me great pain to say this, but...". There was no doubt that his father had been about to reveal the true identity of the head of Minedal-e Corporation.

Then he recalled Tisiphone's last words before she died at the Somtlose, "Rosie was my mother, but she was killed by the police some time ago. Actually, my real name is Tisiphone, not Lucy. Now I'm waiting to be put on trial. The judges have accused me of killing her. They obviously want to frame me. Behind it all is the long arm of that witch from Minedal-e!" And Tisiphone had added, "Some people call her Campe, but no one has ever seen her. The head of the pharmaceutical company isn't Shelton Malthen. He's just a puppet, and someone else is pulling the strings. I don't know any more than that."

David Shelton Malthen too, when he was lying on the floor in his dark blue velvet suit stained with blood, just before dying, said, "Your mother has only ever caused trouble. I am just a pawn, a small tile in a bigger mosaic. Good and evil have always been in balance, and we are the good..."

The conversation he had with Romance also came to mind; when they were at the Rotaon Ltd headquarters at the port of Contempt City he had said, "A while ago one of our spies came back from Africa. In his report he said there was an underground bunker called Tartarus where thousands of vials of EM 0 are produced to be sent to countries in the east. The spy who came back from Africa was named George, and he was the owner of Marleyes restaurant in Surprise City. You've met Stan, his son. For security reasons George kept the first half of the coordinates to reach the MC bunker and then gave the other half to his brother Tim, an eccentric guy with a scruffy beard and long white hair. The coordinates don't only show the whereabouts of the bunker, but also contain a secret message, though no one has ever been able to decipher it."

Now everything started to fall into place and, turning to his mother, William said, "Minedal-e is the anagram of the name Madeline, right? So the letters M and C are not the initials of Minedal-e Corporation, but Madeline Corporation! You are at the head of the pharmaceutical company, isn't that right?"

Madeline stared at him with inexpressive eyes, and her icy face betrayed no emotion whatsoever. It was William who then opened his eyes wide and put his hand to his head as the last details of such a complex reality became clear to him.

"Why didn't I see it before?" said William in a voice trembling with anger, "George knew your identity, that was why you had him killed. For security reasons he kept the first half of the coordinates to himself and then he gave the other half to his brother Tim, the janitor at the Happiness City police station. If I remember correctly the code was: MC = 13 - 1 - 4 - 5 -12N - 9 - 14 - 050E. This not only reveals the coordinates of the bunker, 13°14'51.2"N 9°14'05.0"E, but also the name of the person at the head of

Mined… Madeline Corporation! So the first number of the code, 13, corresponds to the thirteenth letter of the alphabet, which is **M**, the number 1 stands for the letter **A**, 4 is **D**, and 5 is the letter **E**, 12 is **L**, the number 9 corresponds to the letter **I**, 14 to the letter **N** and number 5 to **E**. So each number of the coordinates refers to a letter making up the name Madeline. Incredible! It is your name hidden in the coordinates, and I was a fool not to realize it before now! Poor George had left a very precise message. The numeric sequence was preceded by the letters MC and by the equals sign. George wanted us to know that Minedale Corporation is, equals, Madeline. That is, Madeline is at the head of the entire organization."

"Listen, William…"

"No, you listen to me! When I saw you for the first time in the cell, I knew you were lying. Deceptive expressions are concentrated in the face area, so when a smile is insincere only the area of the mouth is part of the movement, but if it's genuine the whole face lights up because more facial muscles are involved. You were simulating happiness and faking it again and again."

"My son …"

"I am not your son! Do not call me that!"

William jumped up from the chair, but Leonardo was pointing the pistol at his head forcing him to sit down again, and then Madeline began to speak in a solemn tone. "Your father and I loved each other, and we wanted to save the world through our scientific research by crushing illness and eliminating every form of cruelty and hate. As you know, a highly transmissible virus among human beings caused billions of deaths. The pharmaceutical company set up by Paul Shelton Malthen found a vaccine, he mixed it with Em 0 and administered it to all human beings. From that moment on, at the birth of every baby in any part of the world, Em 0 was given to remove any form of emotion. Suddenly wars ceased, crime almost disappeared and human beings were finally free of hate; a new world was born from the previous world's ashes. No one suffered, tears didn't exist anymore."

"I didn't come all this way to hear things I already know," said William angrily.

"Do you want to hear something you don't know?" Leonardo interjected smugly. "It was me who broke into your apartment during the night to take the letter Jacqueline wrote to your father."

"Traitor!" shouted William.

"This defiant temperament is your weak point. not even the academy managed to change you!" cried Leonardo.

"Let me finish. Know your place, Leonardo," said Madeline in an authoritative tone. "Some subjects, like you and your wife Beatrice, seemed resistant to Em 0. Besides, it was becoming hard to produce millions of doses and get them to the remotest parts of the earth. So with David Shelton Malthen and other scientists we developed a hydrosoluble version of Em 0. We carried out tests and the results were positive, and there was then almost no need to inject Em 0 because it was enough to put it into the water supply or hydropower plants, such as that of Fear City."

The words of David Shelton Malthen came to William's mind, "By mixing Em 0 with various substances, forgive me if I don't go into detail by listing them all, as not being an expert you wouldn't understand, we managed to create a hydrosoluble serum. When a schoolteacher, for instance, informed us of a child who appeared to show emotions, we intervened by simply making the child drink a glass of water in which Em 0 was dissolved. In our great magnanimity, we gave everyone a second chance to redeem themselves. Then if the second dose of the serum did not have an effect, we proceeded with the physical elimination of the subject."

Madeline had the tone of voice of someone wanting to free themselves from a great burden, saying, "We didn't agree with David Shelton Malthen because he wanted to go ahead with the physical elimination of all those subjects resistant to a second dose of Em 0, whereas I was convinced that by administering further doses sooner or later the emotions would be extinguished in any person. So, without the knowledge of my colleagues or Dr. David Shelton Malthen, I independently set in motion a secret operation to introduce Em 0 into the main water supplies of large cities. In this way the emotions of the refractory subjects were kept constantly at bay."

"Speaking of David, you will have been informed that he is no longer at MC. I avenged my father and that is enough for me. If you want to kill me, get on with it!" said William in the voice of someone resigned to an inevitable fate.

A world without emotions

The tension was growing between the two and soon it would be impossible to contain.

3.1

Madeline was continuing her explanation. In an irritated tone and with rising anger, she said, "Em 0 was not administered to the whole population at once. Initially the idea was to proceed by degrees, selecting the various emotions. I'll explain better. The names of the cities that you know were not given to them randomly; for instance, using an early version of Em 0 at Anger City, all the emotions were eliminated from people with the exception of anger. Crime skyrocketed in that city, as did murder. People argued in the street for stupid reasons and then killed each other. So Happiness City was created, and its inhabitants were given the chance to experience happiness alone, but contrary to what you might assume, suicides increased exponentially, but it shouldn't surprise because happiness alone is not enough to keep people alive, they also need to experience other emotions."

"Your experiments have killed thousands of innocent people!"

"William, science must progress at any cost! Listen! Sadness City was the greatest failure because its inhabitants could only feel the emotion of sadness, and soon everyone fell into a state of deep depression. Unable to find a reason to continue living, they simply let themselves die. There were no longer any happy events, such as weddings or birthdays, because people spent all day crying. Whereas Contempt City was populated by haughty people who despised others to such an extent that they never spoke to one another. Fairly quickly the place became deserted, a ghost city. Precisely because of the contempt felt for other people, everyone chose to stay at home and never did anything social."

"You've made humans into laboratory guinea pigs. Don't you see that?"

"You're not a scientist, you can't fully understand the reasons we did all this. Now let me finish. At Disgust City all emotions were eliminated with the exception of disgust, but the results obtained were no better with respect to the other cities, because people were disgusted by everything, even food, and the consequences of this were easily imaginable. In a short time, the people stopped buying food, wasted away and let themselves die of hunger."

William was staring at his mother, her words were like blows to his heart, already suffering and exhausted. The woman, without realizing in the least what her son was feeling at that moment, continued, "Then the attempt was made to eliminate every emotion of the inhabitants of Fear City, leaving them only able to experience fear. People were

219

even afraid of touching a handrail on the stairs because they thought it was infected and they could catch a terrible illness. No one drove anymore due to the fear of encountering the unexpected on the streets. The birth rate rapidly dropped to a historical low, for people feared catching viruses by just having children. It was a failure and, here the people of that city chose social isolation; many of them even refused to go to the doctor to be treated and died at home."

At that moment, William understood that his mother had been blinded by her desire to achieve a perfect society. "That's just a utopia. It is diversity itself that keeps human beings going," he thought.

She concluded, "Finally, the people living in Surprise City were left feeling only the emotion of surprise. In this case too, the scientists marked a total failure of the intended plan. The inhabitants were surprised when someone died of old age and did not accept the event as normal and part of life's cycle. During the day they experienced the emotion of surprise so often that they began to develop serious anxiety disorders and heart problems from the adrenaline spikes. Much of the population soon died due to an increase in sudden cardiac arrests."

"You must understand that biological mechanisms cannot be fought."

"You're right, William, but science is useful for proving that irrefutably. Human beings are somehow designed to experience the whole range of emotions. It was understood how every emotion had its specific purpose and necessarily had to coexist with the others. If, for example, you try to eliminate sadness from people's hearts, they can't feel healthy, intense happiness either. The plan to select emotions failed miserably, so it was decided to eliminate them completely from human beings, developing a new version of Em 0."

"How could you manipulate the lives of so many people without feeling an iota of compassion?" William asked, looking her straight in the eye.

"Compassion is a feeling that a leader cannot allow herself. Over time, my brilliant insights in the field of science led me to take over the firm founded by Paul Shelton Malthen, until one day I decided to change the name into an anagram of my own. Your father was an idealist and had a vision of the world totally opposite mine. I was aiming for a perfect world, while he considered reality from a different perspective and thought that human beings without emotions would only turn into zombies. He acknowledged that suffering had disappeared from the world, but he thought it was fundamental for human beings and considered sadness to be a very important emotion, on a par with joy."

"Have we reached the afterword of your love story, Madeline?"

"I admire your sense of humor. At that point, we took different paths, and he founded Emosemvi, declaring war on me, and I continued to carry out my scientific research. When you were born, for safety reasons and because by now there was a constant clash between the resistance and my company, your father and I decided to disappear. He staged a car accident, sending his flaming car into a ditch. The police took him for dead, thinking his body had been carbonized with the metal of the car, while with the help of the hospital doctors, I staged my own death as I gave birth to you."

"It seems the perfect plan, but have you ever once asked yourself what your father Walter felt when he got the news of your death? How could you give him such pain?"

"He did not feel any pain as sadness did not exist in his heart. At any rate, I was acting for the benefit of humanity. It surprises me that you don't understand that. All these years I have always tried to protect you, William. We generally killed subjects who withstood a second dose of Em 0, but you are my son, so we spared your life and the same for your wife. You shouldn't have married because two subjects who are refractory to Em 0 can, with greater ease than others, trigger emotional processes. Administering Em 0 to you both we were convinced that we had removed your memories of your marriage, but time has shown how that was impossible because somehow you always found a way of coming together again. I tried to protect you as long as I could, but then your investigations began to create immense difficulties."

Little by little, Madeline was revealing the weave of the cloth made with the thread of lies, in all its details. "Leonardo was specifically sent to the academy to keep an eye on you. If I remember correctly, on the day of the swearing-in ceremony he suggested you go with him to the police station at Sadness City. If you had listened to him rather than being stubborn like your father, it would all have been simpler because we could have kept close tabs on you. Instead you chose to be assigned to the Happiness City police station. We have fewer infiltrators there, although Chief of Police McMillan and your ex colleague John were both ours.

"They were corrupt!"

"However you want to look at it. They only chose to work for the winning team. At any rate, we had to keep on administering you with Em 0 because emotions still existed in your spirit, and, worse, somehow memories were resurfacing. When you returned home after the swearing-in ceremony, you drank some red wine and the next day you woke up with a terrible headache. This was because the previous night our men had let themselves into your apartment and poured Em 0 into the bottle of wine."

"Friendship..." William whispered sadly.

Leonardo was about to answer, but Madeline glared at him to keep his mouth shut, and she continued, "Then we decided to stage a robbery at your apartment to allow Leonardo to install the video camera in the fireplace. As you got back earlier than expected, you found Leonardo still in the apartment. You spent the evening talking and drinking beer into which Leonardo had poured Em 0.

We also had to stave off Beatrice's emotions and memories too, so at her house we filled every bottle of wine with Em 0, and, if I'm not mistaken, you unknowingly swallowed a dose drinking a toast with her during a romantic dinner. We thought that neither of you remembered being married at all, but she bought the apartment in your very building. This choice was less random than one might think because the place was familiar to her; once, when you were still children, you took her home to your grandfather Walter."

Suddenly, a crackling voice issued from Madeline's small two-way radio, as the head of security in the bunker was asking her if she needed any help. She replied in a sharp tone, "Everything is going according to plan, I'll be back in my office shortly."

She put the two-way radio in her pocket and went on talking. "Where was I? Ah yes, So you were getting too close to the truth and were a threat to my organization. With my heart ripped with pain, I made the decision to have you run over by one of our men, but he didn't succeed in killing you and you ended up in the hospital. While you were there a nurse who works under cover for our organization, by the name of Hygieia, put a dose of Em 0 into your IV. She obviously couldn't kill you in the hospital or there would have been trouble. You noticed a tattoo on Hygieia's arm of a bowl with a snake coiled around it. Beneath it were the stylized letters "M" and "C." You were becoming very suspicious, so you asked her the meaning of the two letters. She told you they were the initials of her husband, Milton Capersson, but they were actually the initials of my pharmaceutical company.

"I remember that nurse. I didn't think your organization would go so far!"

"It took years to grow it, but now we're pretty much everywhere. If I remember right, McMillan also offered you some rum spiked with Em 0 in his office. We were worried because initially you didn't seem to want to drink it, but in the end, you gave in. And the time Leonardo came to pick you up at the Eversten, that dusty old abandoned movie theater, he brought you some water with the serum dissolved in it. At your first meeting with David Shelton Malthen his secretary offered you some water, and now you can imagine why. Then Leonardo came to pick you up at home to take you to the Somtlose and he turned up with some hot coffee spiked with Em 0."

Visibly shaken by what he was hearing, William couldn't stop himself exclaiming, "Friends help each other when they are in trouble! Isn't that right, Leonardo? That's what you said to me when we were at my house! I trusted you!" Leonardo remained impassive as though the words hadn't the slightest effect on him.

Sighing, Madeline went on, "We tried to kill you at the Somtlose too, and that day you should have been blown up in the café, but once again you managed to save yourself. On the one hand, it was a blessing for our organization because you revealed to Leonardo the code the resistance used to communicate. That evening we found out that when two members of the resistance met, they started to refer to the emotions by saying such things as "eating that food makes you happy" or "that music makes you sad." As they said phrases of this type, they expressed the emotions through facial micro-expressions."

"I feel responsible! I was so naive, it's my fault that innocent people died!"

"You're too rash, you should be shrewder and more rational. Anyhow it's an ingenious system because those who are not trained do not notice micro-expressions, so if one of the two speakers is not a member of the resistance, they don't realize what is happening. Thanks to the information you supplied, we started to train our operatives to simulate emotions and use this code. Put simply, our operatives were able to identify and kill the members of Emosemvi. You will have noticed how a wave of violence came over the cities. The people who disappeared were all connected in some way to the resistance, and the places that were blown up belonged to them."

For a moment, William felt his strength fail, for what he was hearing was too much even for someone as strong as he was.

As the air in the room seemed to vibrate like a taut rope, Madeline was coming to the end of her speech. "Then we managed to get our hands on the Reversing serum. I never imagined that the resistance was so well organized, and we were wrong to underestimate it in the past. Thanks to you we have almost completely annihilated Emosemvi and through your ex colleague John we found out about the meeting of the resistance leaders at Gear Jesture."

"You killed innocent people then."

Madeline replied with incomparable coldness, "You should have lost your life on that occasion too at the hands of our men when they stormed the garage, but you managed to get away through the trapdoor in the floor. So you see, I know about everything. Your father's particular organizational touch shows in Emosemvi. Virgilio was a meticulous sort, and he always tried to anticipate what would happen in the future, as though he played chess with destiny trying to calculate every one of his adversary's moves as well. If he had not chosen to leave and fallen in love with that Jacqueline, he would have been a good ally for us, perhaps the best. But he decided to stay in limbo, sighing and never taking decisive action. You can still change the course of fate. Join me, become part of MC and bring continuity to my plan by keeping it going after my death."

William looked at Leonardo with contempt, then he turned to Madeline, saying, "Now you need a successor? How can a wife have her husband killed and want the death of her own son? I feel sorry for people like you. You don't even deserve my disdain. I deceived myself into coming here to give my mother her freedom, and all I found was my executioner! Madeline, your thirst for power has mixed up your mind and deprived you of every emotion, even though they are available to you. With my father, you could have made the world a better place, but instead you have condemned humanity to take a dead-end street. Human beings today no longer have a soul and lack the very love that you should have given to your family."

"You don't understand..."

"No! You don't understand! I'll tell you a secret. When you found out about the code used by members of the resistance to communicate amongst themselves, I imagine you must have been delighted. And yet that was your greatest failure! Do you know why? Because to understand whether a person is or is not in the resistance you just have to look into their eyes. Those who feel emotions have a radiant light in their expressions from the reflections of life! But I don't expect you to be able to understand."

Madeline, her face full of anger, replied, "I could have had you killed on thousands of different occasions. Even when you entered this underground bunker, I could have called security, but I wanted to give you the chance to redeem yourself and make an alliance with me. Your father has led you to embark on a journey with no return, and now we have come to the reckoning!"

Madeline made a gesture to Leonardo, who wore an expression of pure hate. Without thinking twice, he pulled the trigger of his pistol, a flash lit up the walls of the room, immediately after came the roar of an explosion. The bullet followed a straight line into William's shoulder, and he fell onto his side on the floor, the blood began to flow copiously out of the wound, then Leonardo shot again, hitting his left leg. Madeline watched the scene with an imperturbable calm, and at that moment she was celebrating victory in her heart. An entire chapter of her life came to a close that day, and she had just written the words "the end" on the final page.

William looked into his mother's eyes one last time, and he noticed a strange brilliance in her glacial expression. In a part of the heart that had hardened over time, she was feeling compassion for the child she had given life to so many years before and who was now dying. A tear slid out of her eye, and Leonardo pointed at William's head and pulled the trigger one last time. Bam!

Lying on the floor in the room was the body of a man who during his life had believed he was on the side of good: Leonardo exhaled his last breath. He had been hit in the head by the pistol that William had quickly pulled out of the holster at his ankle. Leonardo was killed by the Second Chance! At the academy Leonardo had advised William to keep an extra pistol handy and after all this time the advice turned out to be fatal for him.

Madeline sat petrified for a moment, as she hadn't expected to see one of her best men die in that way. William was losing a lot of blood from his shoulder and leg. His limbs were beginning to go numb and as soon as the last strength he had left was depleted, he would say goodbye to the world and meet Virgilio in the afterlife. He aimed his pistol at Madeline, who cried, "It's over William. Put the gun down!"

Then she quickly reached into her coat to pull out a pistol, leaving William no choice but to fire first, hitting her in the stomach. She fell gasping to the floor, then began to wheeze and to feel the cold breath of death around her neck, at which point she held her hand out to her son. He was in agony due to the wounds he had sustained and very weak from loss of blood, but he slithered across the floor and took her hand. The world around them stopped for a second, even the defective neon light stopped flashing on and off frenetically. The dust was suspended in the air as a guilt-filled mother and a son responsibility for having killed her, looked into each other's eyes as they waited for death to carry them away.

The act of giving life is the gesture of love that holds the secret of the world, and in the mystery of death, lies fate. Sometimes fate plays dice with life and subverts logic to such an extent as to create unlikely situations like the one of the two poor souls lying on the cold floor of the meeting room in an underground bunker.

In an atmosphere heavy with expectation, it was silence that made the most noise. In a whisper of a voice Madeline said, "I'm sorry, my son. All this shouldn't have ended like this. I have met you twice in my lifetime: the first time was when you were born, the second on the day I tried to have you killed. But now something has changed, and I'm sorry for what I have done."

She gave a cough and continued, "Everything makes sense, now I can see clearly, as though I have woken from a long sleep. Human beings deserve to know love and to enjoy its wonders. My heart dried up due to the disappointments of my life, but since I met you today, everything changed... I see a world painted in the colors of hope."

William barely managed to speak the word "Mom" before his eyes closed. His heartbeat was slowing down, and the angel of death was reaching out to him.

Madeline took the two-way radio out of her pocket, but it slipped through her limp, bloody hands. She picked it up and with a last effort called for help. Then everything went black.

4. Playing dice with emotions

"Death has no color, much less a taste or any kind of shape. Even a funeral is not, in itself, a sad event, but it is made sad by the emotions of the people taking part. And yet it is hard to think of death without associating it with pain and tears William was pondering this a moment before being interrupted by jumbled voices.

He opened his eyes and found himself in a hospital bed, next to him, sitting on a metal chair was Orpheus holding his lyre, while two doctors were talking with each other in a corner of the room.

Orpheus saw his friend regain consciousness. "How are you feeling, William?"

"Where am I?"

"In the hospital in Dakar."

"How did I get here?"

"You were hit twice by a firearm. The woman in charge of that bunker radioed the emergency room. She refused to be treated first, ordering the paramedics to help you, and then she died. They tried to revive you. You had lost a lot of blood and were close to death, but thanks to the timely action of the doctors you survived. Fortunately the bullets did not hit any vital body parts. I was at the village organizing the truck when a helicopter landed in the large square. Soon a van arrived, and you were inside lying on a stretcher unconscious. Two men dressed in black carried you into the helicopter and they told me what had happened, then I got in with you and we were brought to the hospital in Burkina Faso. From there another helicopter transferred us to this one."

William felt stabbing pains in his shoulder and left leg where he had been wounded. "I've got to find out how Beatrice is. I have to talk to Romance!"

"Right now, you can't talk to anyone, you must rest."

Resigned, he turned his face to the window, in the distance he could see a lake with pink water; the sun was shining in the frame of the sky turning a solitary cloud red, which stretching itself lazily, seeming to wander aimlessly pushed by a slight breeze. The sight of nature was like salve to his wounds, looking at a beautiful view he felt truly free.

A few days passed and as soon as he was able to walk with the help of a crutch, he asked Orpheus to find a way to get him back to Happiness City. He thought and remembered that two days later the Elpis would be docking at the port of Dakar. William awaited the moment with great anxiety, as he longed to see Beatrice, but he didn't know whether she was still alive. The wait was wearing him out, so he tried to call Romance from a public telephone at the hospital, but, strangely, no one picked up at Rotaon Ltd. "In all likelihood, they captured him and the company headquarters was razed to the ground," he thought sadly.

After two interminable days, Orpheus finally turned up at the hospital and William decided to leave with him and signed the form to discharge himself against the doctors' advice. They took a taxi to the port, the time to say goodbye came and with it some sadness too. William felt in Orpheus' debt and suggested he move to Happiness City, but he refused, saying, "How could I live in the middle of a cement jungle? There are no animals to bewitch with my music. Thank you, but this is my world and I like it here."

"Alright. If I manage to get through all this, I'll come and see you. I owe you my life and I'll never forget all you've done for me."

The two men hugged, then William boarded the ship, where he found the same crew that had accompanied him on his journey out from Contempt City to Dakar. Luckily, in the hold, he also found the coat that he had distractedly left behind.

When the ship was sailing through the middle of the ocean, William found himself in the canteen with Jack, the cook. Though he was a taciturn sort, he was the first to break the silence. "To what do we owe the honor of having you on board our ship again?"

"I'm going home in the hope of holding the woman I love."

"And I got on the ship to forget the woman I love."

"Do you work for Romance?" asked William without beating about the bush.

"No, I do not work for Romance."

"Have you heard of Emosemvi?"

"No, I haven't."

"You don't lie very well Jack, you should practice more."

"What do you mean?"

"When I asked you if you worked for Romance you said no. However, as you did so you rubbed your right eye. Then when I asked if you had heard of Emosemvi again you replied no, but just as you were saying that you crossed your legs."

"So? Those are perfectly natural actions, aren't they?"

"Maybe an untrained eye would judge them as normal, but in fact they are not. During a conversation a human being makes certain gestures, like for example scratching a part of the body or rubbing an eye. These are the very movements that reveal what emotions they're feeling. In our head there is a gland called the amygdala, and its job is to register states of emotional excitement, meaning it sets off a process that regulates cardiac frequency, dilation of the pupils, trembling of the limbs and so on. All of these processes often give rise to physical needs that have to be satisfied in some way. But, when one lies or feels a sense of irritation, one tends to change position on one's chair or scratch specific parts of the body, as happened in your case."

"Interesting!"

"It is! I know the resistance code, but I've modified it a bit, because it takes too long to use the typical lexical expressions referring to an emotional state such as, "I am happy," or "I despise that person," and at the same time show facial micro-expressions. I just talk for a bit to someone and observe their body language. If, by observing small details I realize that the person I'm talking to is experiencing emotions, I am certain that they've injected Reversing."

"You are astute, William! Alright, I'll tell you what I know. Rotaon Ltd was blown up and Romance has disappeared, he might have died in the explosion. Emosemvi is almost completely wiped out, and there are no real leaders who can continue the fight against MC. Everything has changed since Virgilio died, the resistance has begun to slowly split apart, and we need someone who can reorganize it."

"It seems worse than I thought. It can't have been easy for you either."

"It wasn't. I used to run a secret laboratory under a bakery in the center of Disgust City where we managed to produce large quantities of Reversing, and then, like all the other laboratories, it was blown up. MC discovered our communication code and used it against us. Those bastards went into a shop and spoke to the owner using facial micro-expressions so that he believed they were in the resistance; no sooner did they find he was able to feel emotions than they killed him. It was so horrible! I am one of the last Emosemvi specialists who knows how to produce

Reversing, but we are short of laboratories and raw materials."

"There's still a chance... There's always a chance! Virgilio was my father, and the resistance is not completely beaten. We will rebuild what they have destroyed, and we will rise again, but I need to get all the Emosemvi survivors together. The leaders of MC are dead, now is the time to react and fight back hard."

"You're Virgilio's son! Your achievements are becoming legendary among the few survivors of the resistance. They talk of nothing but you and hope you will lead us to victory just as your father did. The blood of a great hero runs in your veins. I believed in your father and I'll believe in you if you will lead us."

"I will do it. I would be honored to lead the resistance. We will give everyone back the chance to feel emotions, so my father won't have died in vain."

"I'm with you! We'll organize a meeting with the other resistance survivors at the Bringlux Hotel in Surprise City. I'll find a way of contacting you with all the details."

"Good, agreed, but as soon as we disembark, I have to go to the hospital at Anger City."

"Do you need a ride?"

"No thanks, I'll go alone. I have to take care of some things there."

After this brief conversation, William nodded goodbye and went back down below. Something had clicked inside him, and he felt he could continue his father's work. The time had come to pay him homage by bringing new hope to the world. His mother Madeline, just before she died, had repented of the evil she had done in the course of her life. If she were still alive, maybe she would have helped her son carry out this task.

The Elpis docked at the port in Contempt City in the late afternoon. Some black clouds in the sky were arrogantly bearing down, irreverently pushing the softer white clouds out of the way, soon their brooding would turn into lightening and a downpour. As soon as he got off the ship, he noticed a heap of rubble from a burnt-out building; the singed wooden sign saying Rotaon Ltd was still standing firm and proud, like a general without an army. For those hanging around the port the heap of rubble meant nothing, while for William it was another reason to continue his fight against the criminal organization.

Avoiding being spotted by the security guards, he left the port walking slowly along with the help of his crutch, as his wounds were still hurting; he found his car exactly where he had left it before leaving for Africa, but he chose to be prudent and keep his distance in order to observe the area closely. The car was covered in dust, but it didn't look damaged; not far off a street vendor was arranging food on a cart, an old woman carrying shopping bags was walking along the sidewalk, and everything seemed quiet.

Suddenly, William noticed a man sitting on some nearby rocks looking through a pair of binoculars at the very area where his car was parked. "If he is just a sea watcher, why aren't his binoculars pointing at the horizon?" William wondered, becoming suspicious; catching a whiff of a trap, he crept down an alleyway making sure he was not seen. After waiting a good while, the opportunity finally came for him to emerge from the alleyway. A long line of trucks had stopped at the entrance to the port so, taking advantage of the cover offered by the vehicles, he managed to get away without being seen by the man with the binoculars.

There was no one he could trust any more. The only friends he had felt attached to in his life were John and Leonardo, both had betrayed him and were now dead. In the hopes that he could hold Beatrice in his arms once again he took a taxi to the Anger City hospital, paid the driver with the little money left in his pocket, then walked into the emergency room. Just as he reached the reception and was about to ask the nurse behind the desk for information, he heard his name.

A television on the wall was showing images of the rubble of Rotaon Ltd and the Somtlose, and the journalist informed the viewers of the painful nature of the tragedy, putting the blame on William, whose apartment the judges had sequestered. He was struck by this fact because the judges were supposed to defend citizens, their freedom and justice. They weren't supposed to attack them and ruin their lives. Sequestering someone's home not only deprived that person of a property, but it was a personal blow. Home has always been a refuge from the chaos of the world, the place, built from sweat, where dreams and hopes for the future of one's children live. With reasoning totally detached from logic, as though it were divine emanation, sometimes the law was used to harm decent people. As these thoughts created turmoil in his mind, he couldn't stop himself exclaiming, "Cowards!" then he added, "You can have my material property, but your laws will never sequester my emotions!"

As he was absorbed in these thoughts, a nurse asked him if he needed any help and as if rousing himself from sleep, he turned towards her and asked which room Beatrice Whites was in. The woman consulted her computer, but no patient of that name was being treated in the hospital; then she checked the discharge log and finally found something. Beatrice had left the hospital in a great hurry the day before. The nurse remembered having seen her leave with a man dressed in black.

"Damn it!" exclaimed William. Beatrice might have been kidnapped, in a flash all his hopes of holding her dissolved like snow in the sun. His heart could not take losing her again. But it wasn't the time to get demoralized. He didn't have much time left so he needed to act fast. William was tired and famished, but he didn't have a dime and his wounds were hurting more and more, so he sat on a bench outside the hospital wondering what to do next.

Evening fell and with it came a biting cold that pierced his body and into his very bones. Right then, William heard someone call his name, he turned and saw a man in a car, looking closer he recognized Jack, the cook he had met on the ship, who said, "I was worried about you, you didn't seem in good shape on the ship. You looked very pale. Do you want a ride?"

"Yes, please, I was freezing."

He got into the car and Jack drove him to the Martin, a nearby restaurant, and bought him dinner, and then they talked of all sorts of things, but not about Emosemvi because there could have been spies around. It was a comfortable place, a bit like a saloon from the Old West. On the walls hung wooden tools that they used to shoe horses in the olden days, and the bar was shaped like a steam train, while, cutting a fine figure right in the middle of the main room was a telescope on a tripod. Jack knew the owner of the spot well. He was named Seamus, his origins were Irish, and he was a friendly type although somewhat awkward in his movements. William did not know whether Seamus was in the resistance or not, and right then he didn't even have the time to watch his face for expressions, because he was famished and was wolfing down a stew.

After dinner they went to Jack's apartment in the suburbs of Fear City. It seemed comfortable place but didn't give the impression of belonging to a person with much money. The spartan furniture and the wallpaper were certainly not in good condition, and outside the window there was a neon sign flashing intermittently. Jack said he saved a lot of money on electricity because it provided him with all the light he needed.

They sat on a couch and talked about how useful it was for a human being to feel emotions. Jack had no idea about the mechanisms at the basis of emotions, but he admired their complexity and perfection, and he was impressed by his friend's knowledge and could have listened to him for hours. For his part, William loved talking about such things because he had a natural predisposition for catching the micro-expressions on the faces of the people he talked with.

He explained to his friend how emotions, besides having the function of regulating the state of mind, could also arise from empathy. "Let's imagine having lost a loved one not long ago and assuming a sad expression as we talk with a friend about it. In all probability, the person we are talking with would perceive our pain and in turn would assume the same sad expression. Even though only one of the two has actually lost someone they loved, the emotions are transmitted by empathy, which is, in short, the instinctive capacity to perceive the state of mind of another."

"So if I wanted to induce the emotion of happiness in a friend, I just simulate being happy and show it on my face?" asked Jack.

"It's not as easy as that because there are various factors to consider, besides it is never easy to simulate feeling emotions, it takes a lot of training. We must never forget how a facial expression is just a small tile in a bigger mosaic, so it is the sign that is added to others before one can draw any conclusion."

"You remind me of your father Virgilio. He was a learned and wise person, and according to him knowledge could lead us out of these dark centuries."

"Yes, but I have made a big mistake and obviously I am not as wise. I foolishly put my faith in a guy called Leonardo, telling him about the code that the resistance use to communicate. He actually worked for MC and the mistake destroyed all my father's work and cost the lives of many people. I am the cause of Emosemvi's collapse!"

"We all make mistakes, you won't go to hell for that, and it's not your fault that they betrayed you. Now go and rest because you need it."

It was late, Jack said goodnight to his friend and went into his bedroom, William stretched out on the couch, where he spent the night dreaming of Beatrice. Wearing a splendid ivory wedding dress, she was radiant with happiness and lit up the world with her smile.

5. The dichotomy of light and shadow

Jack was out running errands and had left William at his apartment, where he spent the entire day going through what had happened up to that moment. He was detoxifying from Em 0 and very slowly his memories were beginning to resurface in his mind like spurts of water from an arid land.

He remembered that the first time he saw Beatrice was at elementary school, when they were the same age and too young to understand love. All the same, when class was over, he waited for her at the school gates to walk her home. During the summer break William climbed over the wall of the parish center next to Beatrice's house, hoping to be able to watch her playing in the garden. The two children felt an innocent mutual interest, and even then, the dawn of love had lightly nudged them, awakening their hearts.

They became adults and the vague mutual attraction felt as children finally blossomed into love. Unable to explain why their hearts beat harder when they were together, they were confused, because in the world where they lived no one had ever talked with them about emotions. One summer's day they went to the banks of the River Lethe to see a field of sunflowers in bloom. From there they could admire a magnificent landscape, on one side the expanse of sunflowers stretching beyond the horizon, on the other the majestic town of Anger City. The contrast between nature and the work of human hands was powerful yet seemed to coexist nicely here.

Beatrice was walking along with her face raised as if she wanted to make every ray of sun her own, while William was gazing towards the horizon. Little by little they reached a wide dirt road, unaware of what the future had in store for them; then, they came to a grandiose abandoned windmill, whose blades still moved, turned by the breeze. Just beneath the windmill they exchanged promises of love, and for an instant the world around them lost intensity, the colors of the sunflowers went opaque, the windmill became very small and the rays of the sun turned into those of a distant star; that day their hearts became synchronized and began to beat as one.

The two young lovers continued to walk until they came across some metal drums piled in the middle of the sunflower field. Going closer to see whether they were full of fertilizer or something else to help the plants grow, to their great surprise they realized the drums were full of industrial waste. Neither of them had any idea why the drums were there, but the environment would certainly have been affected by them. In that moment they became aware of how every human being had the duty to leave a better and cleaner world to future generations.

William was letting himself be carried away by the overwhelming power of memories when the telephone rang, bringing him back to reality. He lifted the receiver and put it to his ear, but out of caution he didn't say a word, because it could have been the men from MC calling. But it was Jack. "How are you feeling?"

"Fine, thanks. Today I can walk without the crutch, though the wounds still hurt."

"I've left some money on the sideboard in the kitchen in case you need it. I'm very busy today, let's meet at 10:00 p.m. at the place I told you about on the ship."

"OK, Jack, thanks for everything, see you later."

He trusted Jack, but he wanted to be careful because in the past his two best friends had betrayed him.

As soon as it was evening, he picked up the money from the sideboard in the kitchen and took a taxi to the Bringlux in Surprise City. An eccentric architect had built the hotel a long time before and now it needed renovation. The building was clad in red brick, the facade painted with flames whose coils intertwined to form the letters of the word "Bringlux." The building's shape looked very much like an upside down funnel, with the wide base on the ground and the narrow end pointing up to the sky and it had nine floors with an oddly inconsistent number of rooms; for example, the seventh floor only had three large rooms, while the eighth had ten and the ninth floor had four. From the outside, the hotel seemed quite old and William expected to find it the same inside, but, that day he realized how wrong he was to have preconceptions and jump to hasty conclusions. The lobby was not very large, seemed clean, and was well-lit because a skylight stretched vertically up the whole of the hotel's funnel structure, bringing moonlight down to the lowest floors.

At reception, a transparent counter, much like a large cube of ice in shape and luminosity, there was a middle-aged man wearing a very elegant black suit with a white tie. He was a dashing sort, with smoldering eyes, dark hair and scarlet lips. William got in line behind a few other people to speak to the receptionist, who was just then talking with a blond woman wearing a red dress with a low neckline. She was complaining about her room on the second floor, saying that the air conditioning was so strong that she couldn't even sleep. She was saying to the receptionist, "That infernal blast of air nearly knocked me over, it's an absolute gale. I hope you can send someone up to repair it!" She was clearly exaggerating the matter to make her discomfort clear. William thought how difficult it was to work with clients, how sometimes you meet disrespectful people who feel they have the right to flout the laws of common decency just because they are paying for a product or service.

When the blond woman had moved away, the receptionist turned straight to the next guest in line. He was a middle-aged man, noticeably overweight and wearing an orange robe. He had only just finished eating a snack and with chocolate around his mouth told the receptionist, "The carpet in my room is all muddy, and the shower is so cold that it's like icy rain." In this case too, the receptionist was very patient and obliging, moving the man to another room also on the third floor.

The receptionist saw to the third and last guest in line, who told a story verging on the unbelievable. He was dressed in what remained of a well-tailored suit that was now reduced to tatters and, though he owed the hotel, he said that he had no money because he had spent it elsewhere. Then he added, "I was walking just outside the hotel when some dogs chased and mauled me, scratching my arms and ruining my suit. I hope you don't mind if I settle my account another time." The receptionist seemed to understand fully the guest's distress and allowed him to delay payment. He handed him the key to his room on the seventh floor and said goodbye with great cordiality.

Finally, it was William's turn, the receptionist did not seem upset by the experiences he'd had with the previous guests. "Hello, my name is Bringlux. How can I help you, sir?"

"Hello, Bringlux is your name? Is your name the same as the hotel?"

"Yes, sir, and I am the owner of this place. I expect you are wondering why I am working on reception rather than in an office seated in a luxurious armchair. I'll satisfy your curiosity because I don't want to leave you in any doubt. I am a meticulous person and like to take care of every little detail of my job. If I didn't, the guests would not come back to stay, some are so pleased with the service that they have chosen our hotel as their permanent residence. Others, as you will have noticed observing those ahead of you in line, would like to leave us. But in the end, we always find a way to make them stay. We are extremely kind people."

"It seems to me that your guests are satisfied and happy," agreed William.

"You are using the Emosemvi code, aren't you?"

"Sorry, what?"

"William, I know why you are here."

"How do you know my name? I don't think I told it to you."

"Now you are being simple. Try not to ask obvious questions, however, I'd like to satisfy your curiosity once more. Knowing everyone and everything is part of my job; I hope this doesn't surprise you. Since the world was infected with Em 0, here at the hotel things started to go wrong."

Then the man drew close to William as if he didn't want to be heard by anyone else and whispered, "There is a terrible crisis, and we have even had to close some of the floors of the hotel because of a lack of guests. However, you may stay without paying if you wish. I have a room available on the first floor. It is the one your father liked best."

"In all probability, Bringlux is one of the resistance leaders, and clearly, he had known my father in the past," thought William as he wondered whether or not to trust that man. "Thank you for the offer, but I can't accept. I am here to see a friend."

"In the future, I will make you an offer that you can't refuse, but in the meantime, you can meet Jack and the others in the boiler room. To get there you take the elevator, insert the key in the lock on the panel and press -2."

He thanked the eccentric gentleman, took the key and headed for the elevator.

5.1

The speakers in the elevator were playing rock music. William vaguely remembered having heard it before. The singer was maybe named Michael Lee, but he wasn't sure. The elevator trip was brief, then the doors opened onto a hallway, leading to a room with a large boiler from which issued the seven colored pipes of the heating system.

There were several people in the dimly lit room and, despite the feeble light coming mainly from the boiler flames reflected on the walls, William realized he knew them all. He saw Tobias the old farmer he had met at Gear Jesture, who on seeing William arrive raised the ear trumpet he used to help his deafness in a sign of welcome. To his left was Seamus, the owner of the Martin restaurant and his wife Maggie, who worked at Rotaon Ltd. Sitting on a wooden bench was Stan, son of the late George, and next to him sat his uncle Tim, the janitor at the Happiness City police station. Squatting on the ground was the homeless man to whom William and Beatrice, outside their apartment building, had given a wool coat some time before. In a corner of the room was a man with a patch over his left eye and looking at him more closely William realized it was Willy, captain of the Elpis. Next to him smiling with his lyre was Orpheus, while Jack was slightly further away leaning a shoulder against the wall.

The flame from the boiler seemed to waken for a moment from its torpor, dancing with greater liveliness, its reflections fluttering about on the walls of the room and increasing the intensity of light. Just at the moment when dark met light and caressed it before vanishing, William's heart missed a beat. Before him was a woman with a pink dress and the face of an angel: Beatrice! The two of them melted into an embrace so intense that the flames of the boiler flared up as though someone had thrown on a bundle of wood woven with the feeling of love.

Beatrice looked him in the eye. "Romance got me out of the hospital and away from the MC men who wanted to kill me. He spent days sitting on a chair watching over me. At first, everything seemed to go well, then a nurse came into the room to make my bed and change the IV. I was suspicious because she had a tattoo of a bowl with a snake coiled around it and the two stylized letters "M" and "C." Romance realized it too and threw me a glance to warn me of danger, then he grabbed the arm of the nurse, who in the meantime had taken a syringe out of her pocket and he flung her to the floor. As she fell, she hit her head and was confused for a while. We took advantage of that to run out of the room and leave the hospital. How are you? What happened to you?"

"I'm fine, my love, and a million words wouldn't be enough to describe what happened to me. You are alive and I want nothing more. I love you and I have always loved you, since we were children. I don't know if your memories are gradually coming back, but I remembered meeting you for the first time in the school classroom; at the time I was only a child and I didn't know why my heart leapt when I saw you: all these years later it still happens."

Beatrice nodded, deeply moved, then William added, "If we want the chance to live our love freely, we must act quickly and win the fight against MC."

A man walked out of the shadows, he wore a brown coat with a fur collar and William recognized Romance and went over to shake his hand with great feeling, thanking him for saving Beatrice's life.

In a solemn tone Romance said, "I imagine you know everyone already. Old Tobias feigned death and escaped the attack at Gear Jesture, I had given him up for dead and yet here he is. Unfortunately his son didn't make it that evening. I escaped from Rotaon Ltd just in time before they blew it sky high. I tried to contact you but couldn't. Each of us has honored the promise to your father; he asked all the members of Emosemvi and their families to protect you, and we have tried to do that as well as we could, maybe you'll excuse us if sometimes we haven't fully succeeded, like the time they tried to run you over with the car."

Indicating the homeless man with his hand, he went on, "James was following you and was on the other side of the street in the van where he lived when he saw the red Whilson without plates run you over while you tried to cross the street to join your colleague John. James couldn't do anything to help you that time, and we all feared for your safety. Jack told me how MC found out about the resistance communication code, but you shouldn't feel guilty because that traitor Leonardo deceived you. Initially the members of the resistance at Happiness City and the nearby towns numbered about a thousand. Unfortunately, the people in this room are the only survivors of MC's total massacre of our people."

"I still feel guilty. Thank you for what you are saying, your words give me strength."

"I am always sincere, you will have realized by now. You should know that recently the police forensics team went to Dr. David Shelton Malthen's office to examine the room and gather more evidence. One of our men infiltrated in the team was right there. When no one was looking he managed to steal some documents from a folder lying on the desk. On a wall of the room there was an open safe, where the file had clearly been kept. Reading the documents in the file, our man made an incredible discovery."

William was listening attentively to Romance who continued his account, adding details, "The history books say that Dr. Paul Shelton Malthen discovered a cure for the Coris-91 virus, but that is a lie, the truth is completely different and had been hidden inside a safe until our man infiltrated in police forensics discovered it."

"I'm starting to guess what happened, but tell me, I'm still curious."

"Well, Dr. Paul Shelton Malthen developed the terrible Coris-91 himself, then went to the market in Fear City and dropped a glass vial containing the lethal virus on the ground. Not long afterwards, people started to get sick and just when billions of people had lost their lives, the astute Paul brought out the vaccine, and from that day on he got rich and was honored as the savior of humanity. The truth was hidden from the entire world, which is why there are still those today who kneel at the feet of the many statues of Dr. Paul."

William was quiet for a moment, finally the complete mosaic had taken shape in his head, all the pieces now fitting to perfection.

It was the time to act quickly, so in a solemn tone, he said, "Friends, I thank you from the depths of my heart for being here. I'll be honest with you. At first, I didn't want to side with the resistance. I wanted a life that was normal and problem free, but then I realized that normal does not exist. It's just an excuse for those who don't know how to make their lives better. Avoid normal or you will chase after it all your life and when you have seized it you will realize it has no substance. In life I have learned that problems do not solve themselves; if you really want something you have to fight until you get it. My father created Emosemvi, he freed many people with Reversing, and he died clinging to a piece of hope. We have all received it from his hands, otherwise we would not be in this room today!"

The leader in him was finally coming out.

"Many years from now, when I only have a few minutes left to live, I don't want to look back and regret not at least having tried to change things. The uncommitted never act for good or bad in their lives , but I am not like that, we are not like that, because otherwise today we would be sitting comfortably on the couch at home watching our children with an inexpressive face and blank stare. But today we are claiming the right of free men, capable of feeling emotions and of crying, laughing and dreaming!"

The attentive expressions of everyone there said more than words could: these people would follow him to hell and back. Just like his father, William was able to touch the hidden chords of people's hearts with his words.

After a short pause, he resumed his talk with more urgency, "Tomorrow we will launch operation 'Purgatory' with the aim of giving every human being the chance to experience emotions. This will be like purifying their souls, which is why the operation has the code name of 'Purgatory.' So we will not act in an underhand way like MC, but we will give each person the chance to choose whether to inject Reversing, or to keep everything in their life just as it is, and to leave emotions out of their heart. We will fight a war without killing anyone. We will not leave a long trail of blood behind us, we are not MC! We will use the much more powerful weapon of free information."

Everyone clapped their hands enthusiastically, their mood now fervent.

"MC controls social media, and we can't publish a video without it being immediately censored, so we will use the old-fashioned way by printing material for our publicity. Tomorrow morning Stan, Tobias, James and Willy will go to Marleyes to pick up the ink, paper and the mass printing machine, spending as little time there as possible, because the place might be being watched by MC. Then they will go to the port at Contempt City and on the ship Elpis they will start producing hundreds of flyers printed with the following message: "Emotions are not a legend. The time has come to get them back! Minedal-e Corporation is depriving you of freedom, taking away your right to smile at life. Tomorrow at 8:30 p.m. tune in to the national news channel and you will know the truth." Then they will add the slogan, "The cure is in emotions. Don't be made to conform." Don't forget to print the Emosemvi logo, the white mask with the three red tears on the flyers too."

"Who are we going to distribute the flyers to?" Stan asked with a serious expression.

"As soon as the material is printed, you will go to Fear City University to distribute them among the students. Young people know how to use technology, and in a few hours, they'll use their cell phones to share our message with thousands of people, setting up a media sensation of such huge proportions that not even the powerful technological means available to MC will be able to stop it. As soon as you have finished the work at the university, you will come back here. The next day at 8:00 p.m. you must be at the power plant at Sadness City to deactivate the power for the entire city. The blackout will last about two minutes because then the emergency generators will start operating. Soon I will explain why it is important to complete this mission to deactivate the power. So, to sum up, you will pull off two operations. One will see you in action tomorrow first on the ship Elpis and then at the university, while the other will take place the day after tomorrow at the power plant at Sadness City at 8:00 p.m. Your group will use the code name BT. Is everything clear?"

Stan, Tobias, James and Willy nodded, so William continued to illustrate the plan.

"Tomorrow morning, Seamus, Maggie and Tim, will infiltrate the hydropower plant at Fear City and sabotage it so as to interrupt the flow of Em 0 into the water mains. The plant serves most of the nearby towns and your job is of fundamental importance. If you manage to stop the water contamination tomorrow morning, many citizens already resistant to Em 0 will begin to experience emotions and will be more inclined to accept the television message that I'm about to tell you about. Your group has the code name J."

Everyone again made clear that they had understood what their boss had said.

"The day after tomorrow, I will go with Orpheus, Jack, Romance and Beatrice to the Erme national television center in Sadness City to send a powerful message to the population. We'll inject a volunteer with Reversing and use the television cameras to broadcast the images live, showing the effects to the viewers. Thanks to the two-minute power cut organized by the BT group, the Erme building will be in darkness; even the emergency generator won't be activated in such a short time. In those two minutes, taking advantage of the chaos brought on by the blackout, my group will enter the building and barricade ourselves inside the television studios and the studio control room. The code name for our group will be O."

Romance spread out his arms and in a disconsolate voice, said, "Great, William has taken over from his father. Best case scenario, we're goners."

Everyone laughed and the tension about the upcoming risky mission eased.

William waved his hand to ask the others to be quiet so he could resume what he was saying.

"Clearly, we must expect them to put up a lot of resistance at the Erme center because the distribution of our flyers will alert the men from MC, and they will certainly set up an ambush for my team, but we will be smarter than them. For security reasons I prefer not to reveal the full details of the O group's operation. Stan will lead the BT group, while Tim leads the J group. I have just given you all general instructions to carry out your operations. We have been betrayed countless times by our own friends and brothers, so you'll forgive me if I have only given the broad outline of the plan without going into the details."

"Smart choice!" Romance exclaimed.

"Thanks," William replied with a smirk, adding, "When the three operations are accomplished, if all goes well, we will meet back here at the hotel. No one knows if this plan will work, and the risk of loss of life is very high for each of us. It is not too late to back out, our organization is based on freedom of thought and equality, so feel free to choose whether to go back home or take part in this operation."

There was silence in the room, they all looked into each other's eyes as they waited for someone to speak. It was Orpheus who broke the silence, "I will stand by you to the end," then Willy repeated Orpheus's words, as did all the others, one by one.

Although William's plan was clear to all, no one knew how to put it into practice and yet asking questions just then wouldn't have helped anyone, they each had to find solutions, and everyone there would do so on their own.

By now the meeting was over and everyone headed for the lobby of the Bringlux where the eccentric owner of the hotel was waiting for them.

6. The field of poppies

Bringlux led the members of the resistance to a room where the walls were covered in white leather, a large crystal chandelier with incandescent light bulbs hung from the ceiling, and on the floor was a large oriental carpet with the letter "Y" woven into the middle. It was a bare space with almost no furniture, only a clear glass case to keep the dust from the crystal glasses and a wooden cup inside. The smell of incense filled the air though there was no sign of an aroma diffuser.

Bringlux held his face a few inches from a minuscule retinal scanner then out of the wall came a small keyboard, and he keyed in the code: "2522Y." The walls of the room flipped over, turning back to front and revealing something incredible. On a rack was an orderly display of various automatic guns and to the left were about a hundred vials of Reversing inside clear plastic boxes. Beneath them were some two-way radios, smoke bombs and plastic explosives. With a touch of pride in his voice, Bringlux said, "This is my small personal collection, and it is at your service for your 'Purgatory' mission."

Then he went up to William and whispered in his ear, "Don't take it the wrong way but the name of the operation is a bit predictable. I would have chosen something better."

"How do you know about that? Were you listening to us?" asked William with an expression of surprise on his face.

"As I told you, knowing everything about everyone is part of my job. I'm offering you help, and you would do well to accept it. Tomorrow morning you will find this gear distributed among some black bags that you can pick up from the checkroom of the hotel.

I am not a great supporter of MC because since they decided to give that serum to all human beings, my hotel business has gone downhill. You must restore the balance of the world because a human being deprived of emotions is an empty box without a soul. Everyone has the right to choose whether to laugh or cry, whether to sin or do good... put simply: free will has been lost."

The members of the resistance nodded to show they agreed with accepting the help Bringlux offered. Then William said, "Thank you for your help, though we don't plan to kill anyone, we'll still take the weapons to defend ourselves."

They left the room and went to the hotel rooms offered free of charge by the hotel owner. Some slept heavily because they were very tired, while others, despite having had a busy day and being exhausted, preferred to stay awake all night.

The next day, the BT group was the first to leave the hotel for Marleyes in a car with false plates to pick up the kit needed to print the flyers. Stan went into Marleyes with Tobias while James and Willy stayed in the car. Inside the restaurant everything was exactly as Stan had left it and there was no sign of the men from MC. Still lying on the floor was the piece of metal piping that Stan had used to hit William on the day they first met. Tobias and he loaded the trunk of the car with several reams of paper, a manual printer and some packs of colored ink then they drove to the port at Contempt City. They showed the security guards at the entrance a bill of lading provided by Romance and were let through without a problem. Everything seemed to be going well. Followed by the others, Willy made for the Elpis and then the cockpit, but as he opened the door, he found something unexpected. The chief of police of Happiness City Richard McMillan with two uniformed policemen were there waiting for them. A frost settled in the cockpit, and then McMillan said, "Come on in, we've been expecting you!"

Meanwhile, the J group was outside the fence of the hydropower plant at Fear City. No one seemed to be around with the exception of the security guard at the entrance to the place.

Before being employed as a janitor at the Happiness City police station, Tim worked for an electrical maintenance company and had once repaired a fault caused by a short circuit in this very hydropower plant. He couldn't claim to know it well, but some areas were still familiar to him, and he was able to lead the group to the room in which the water was mixed with Em 0 before being released into the city's water mains. With a pair of wire cutters, Seamus cut a hole in the wire fence for him, Tim and Maggie to get through. The guard at the entrance was too far away to be aware of their presence, so they made their way undisturbed to the main building. Tim opened a metal door and led the others along a corridor full of pipes to the door of the plant control room. He was carrying a rifle and was quite proficient at handling it because as a boy he had trained at the firing range several times.

When he was young, he had dreamed of becoming part of the police force, but then his dream vanished when his daughter Claire died of a blood disease, diagnosed too late by the hospital doctor. From that day Tim decided not to bother with his physical appearance anymore, letting his beard and hair grow. Ironically, after changing his job several times, he found the job of janitor at the police station at Happiness City; there he met Stuart and, after injecting himself with Reversing, he chose to join the resistance.

Seamus and Maggie were also carrying rifles, but they hadn't the slightest idea how to use them because they both came from peaceful farming families in Ireland. Tim touched the door handle of the control room, then he turned back to his two friends and said, "The hydropower plant should have been empty today, but outside there are some vehicles belonging to the maintenance technicians, so

I'll have to change the original plan. Behind this door we will find two technicians from the water company, and we won't even lay a finger on. We'll capture them and take them with us to a safe place, then after twenty-four hours we will release them. Before leaving here we must do one last thing, but we'll talk about it later. Questions?"

Seamus and Maggie made gestures to indicate they understood the plan. They both wanted to give the impression that they were up to the job they'd been assigned, but they were both full of fear and definitely not sure they could do it. Tim pushed down the door handle with force, bursting into the control room. Bam! A gunshot exploded and hit the ceiling and in a second Tim's plan crumbled like a sandcastle hit by the waves of a stormy sea.

The first to drop their weapons to the floor were Seamus and Maggie, followed a moment later by Tim. Behind the door to the control room with guns leveled at them were two men from MC. All hope seemed lost, but if at least William had managed to get into the news broadcasting studios and send the message to the population on air, maybe there would be hope for the world. For the members of the BT and J groups, on the other hand, the chances of survival were very slim.

6.1

William tried to contact Stan and Tim via radio to hear how their operations were proceeding, but neither of them answered. Despite the risk of being intercepted, he tried to call them with a cell phone, but he couldn't reach them that way either. Something had gone wrong for both groups, but nonetheless William had decided to go ahead with the plan, and the next day somehow, he and his group would storm the national television center at Sadness City.

He spent the day with Orpheus, Jack, Romance and Beatrice planning every detail of the operation and even trying to predict any likely countermoves by the enemy.

By now evening had fallen and the hopes of seeing his friends were as distant as the stars in the sky. At one point the cell phone rang, and William quickly replied, "Hello!"

"It's McMillan. An international warrant for your arrest is on your head. Four criminals on the ship Elpis were planning subversive activities, but fortunately we now have them in custody. They have all confessed and we are aware of your intentions; it's over, you must surrender to the authorities. It's really too bad, you were a good cop and had a brilliant future ahead of you."

"Corruption is what's too bad. I trusted you! MC is on borrowed time and so are its collaborators. You've got nothing on us, nothing!"

William hung up because soon the police specialists would be able to trace the phone signal and find his whereabouts.

Beatrice had heard the phone conversation and seeing William visibly shaken, she went up to comfort him, but he was too tense and left the hotel for a breath of fresh air and to calm down a bit. Romance joined him. "Is there a spy amongst us? How did MC know our movements beforehand?"

"You think there's a spy. Who could it be? Right now, I don't even want to think about it. I've been betrayed so many times in my life. I'm exhausted!"

"Maybe we should change our plans, Will. I heard your conversation with that cop, and if he's telling the truth they'll set a trap for us at the Erme television center in Sadness City. It would be suicide to go there and it would be the end of Emosemvi."

"The plan doesn't change, Romance. We'll do what we decided."

"They'll kill us all! There weren't many of us before we lost the BT group, now there are even fewer. Maybe we should surrender!"

"Surrender?"

"Yes, maybe we should negotiate a surrender and try to save our friends' lives."

William looked up at the moon, hoping to find in its pure white rays the inspiration needed to do the right thing.

Meanwhile Seamus, Maggie and Tim were handcuffed to a metal pipe in a room at the hydropower plant. In their hearts was the deep sadness of having failed in their attempt. The world wouldn't change at all. The resistance had been almost completely wiped out, and by now MC had won its battle. The door opened and a thin man with a thick red beard, blue eyes and large square glasses came in, carrying a pistol and limped conspicuously, as though he had a problem with his left leg. As soon as she caught sight of him Maggie closed her eyes and started to pray, the man with the red beard pointed his pistol at Tim's temple and told him to get ready to die, though first he had to make a phone call to an old friend; he used the cell phone to call William who was still staring up at the starry sky, lost in thought. At the first ring he answered, "Yes?"

"It's Peter, remember me?"

"I remember sparing your life in Shelton Malthen's office."

"That was a mistake and to help you see why I'm going to tell you a little story. When I was a boy I used to go hunting with my father. Once, not far from home, I wounded a wolf with my rifle by mistake. At first, I wanted to spare its life, but my father advised me to kill it because that very wolf might come back to our house one day and tear us to pieces. That day I learned never to give anyone a second chance. You made the mistake of giving one to me and as you see I've come back."

"What do you want?"

"Mission hydropower plant has failed miserably. I'll make a deal. I will let your two friends go, and, in return, you turn yourself in to us. What do you think?"

"I've got three friends, not two."

"You're right, sorry. I'm no good at math."

Peter aimed his pistol, pulled the trigger and shot Tim in the back, who fell to the ground without a word. The sight made Maggie start to cry while Seamus turned his face to the wall.

"I'm getting better at math, I was right, wasn't I? You've got two friends. You come alone and unarmed to the hydropower plant at Fear City. It would be a shame to have to kill your other two friends." Peter ended the conversation, putting the cell phone back in his pocket, and he left the room slamming the metal door behind him. Just at that moment, as if the terrible noise of that door had delivered the final blow to Tim, he let out his last breath with the name of his daughter Claire on his lips.

William went back inside the hotel. Orpheus asked him what had happened, and he answered that he had to go to the hydropower plant to save his friends. Though Romance, Jack and Beatrice advised him against going alone and unarmed, he wouldn't listen to reason. He wore the sad expression of a soldier returning home after losing the war, and right then he just wanted to get it over with. He asked his friends not to follow him, put his pistol on the table and left. Beatrice ran after him, trying to persuade him to change his mind, but Romance took her arm beseeching her to respect William's decision. As she tried to pull free of Romance, she yelled, "No! They'll kill him, stop!" But it was too late because he had already disappeared behind the door to the elevator to go down to the hotel garage.

He took Jack's car and drove to the hydropower plant, at the main gate the security guard and two men from MC signaled for him to get out of the vehicle with his hands up. He didn't even put up resistance when they frisked him without finding a weapon, and then they took him to the place where Seamus had used the wire cutters to get through the fence. Peter was there waiting for him with the two handcuffed hostages. Looking over his shoulder through the corner of his eye William realized he had been followed by the men from Minedal-e Corporation, while the security guard had stayed to stand guard at the entrance to the plant.

Peter turned to William, "Today we are celebrating the end of the resistance. Minedal-e Corporation is like a phoenix that always rises from its ashes, whereas the resistance is like a movie without a plot or an audience wanting to watch it. Because of you I can't walk properly. You remember shooting me in Dr. Shelton Malthen's office, don't you? And yet you spared my life but though I cannot do the same for you and your friends because I must carry out my orders, I will kill you quickly."

"It surprises me that you are so cruel to the person who spared your life. I am not a killer, and, despite everything, I would save your life even now, because people like you deserve prison, and I wouldn't assume the right to take the life of another human being unless it was absolutely necessary."

Just then, Orpheus, Jack, Romance and Beatrice leaped out of a large bush on the other side of the fence. Quickly stepping through the hole made by Seamus beforehand, they pointed their guns at the backs of the men from MC, making them surrender. Peter was speechless, his eyes were wide with disbelief, and then he threw his pistol to the ground and raised his hands. Orpheus took a bug detector out of his pocket similar to the one Tim had given to William some time before at the police station at Happiness City, and said, "Next time hide your bugs better! If it were up to me, I'd kill you on the spot for what you did to Tim!"

When William had gotten Peter's call at the hotel, he had been aware of the bug sewn into the cuff of the red satin lining of his coat for some time. He had agreed with his friends to use the bug against their enemies by leading them astray and Peter's call seemed to him the perfect opportunity for the setup. Beatrice had actually known about everything and had pretended to be tortured by William's decision to give himself up to Peter.

The resistance took a first victory that day, though Tim's death saddened the hearts of everyone. Unfortunately things were not going well for the BT group. Stan, Tobias, James and Willy were locked in a cold cell at Happiness City police station. The operation had failed and corrupt police officers, working for Minedal-e Corporation, had beaten them up to extort information and make them confess. Contrary to what McMillan had told William during their last phone call, no member of the BT group had revealed anything. They would rather have died than betray Emosemvi.

William took Seamus and Maggie's handcuffs off and they both flung on him to hug him excitedly. Copious tears of joy mixed with pain poured from their eyes. On the one hand they were happy to be free, but on the other they felt great sadness at Tim's death.

The two men from MC, Peter and the security guard at the entrance, who in the meantime had been taken prisoner, were handcuffed in the room where Tim had been killed; his body was buried by his friends in a grave dug not far from there in a field of poppies.

In that season the poppies shouldn't have been flowering and yet they were there with their slender stalks, as if to be spectators to the unusual events that were happening in the world.

In the shade of those flowers with their intense smell, his friends sent Tim their final heartfelt farewell, wetting the ground with their bitter tears, which ran down their cheeks picking up the speed to leap down to the earth. Then the sun made them evaporate and, once they reached the sky in the form of droplets, they would condense again to fall back down to earth. Their tears would then join Tim who thanks to those tears imbued with the emotions of his friends, would have them near him for some time longer.

The group made their way to the control room at the hydropower plant. On a large panel covered in buttons and warning lights, there was a lever to turn off the dosage of

Em 0. William pulled it downwards, the sound of gear wheels followed by a deep silence was greeted by all present with joy, and right then the mixing process of Em 0 with water was brought to a halt: the hope of being able to smile was becoming a little more real for human beings!

William turned to his friends, "We'll position explosive charges at every door in the hydropower plant. The security guards will soon find them and call the bomb disposal specialists. At least two days are needed to clear the entire building, which is enough to keep Em 0 clear of the local population's homes and let us complete our mission."

After placing the last explosive on the door to the hydropower plant control room, the members of the J and O groups returned to the hotel. Their thoughts were with their friends being held prisoner by the police, for now there was no way they could rescue them, and they had very little hope of seeing them again.

7. The world in color

The following day William didn't want to see any of his friends. As evening strode forward quickly, overtaking the afternoon and leaving it behind, Beatrice decided to go and talk to him. She told him that right then he was the will of all the remaining members of Emosemvi, each of them would follow him all the way to hell if necessary but storming the Erme television center would be outright suicide, so they thought the plans should be changed.

He shook his head and said, "I gave everyone the chance to opt out, if anyone wants to leave, they are free to do so. Whoever wants to stay must be ready at 7:00 p.m., the plan stays as it is."

At the agreed time he went down to the hotel lobby and all the members of Emosemvi were there waiting for him. No one had backed out, they would follow their leader to the end, like a cavalry regiment charging a firing squad. But looking closer, Romance was missing and there was no sign of him in the lobby. Maybe he had decided to opt out, but no one could blame him for that. Then the sound of a car horn echoed through the lobby and a white van came to a halt outside the hotel with Romance at the wheel waving at his friends to come on out. He hadn't backed out either!

Once they had loaded the automatic rifles and the rest of the gear in the back, the group got into the van and headed at breakneck speed for the Erme national television center in Sadness City. The police force and men from MC had been positioned around the building for two hours already. Snipers were deployed on the surrounding roofs, while MC operatives in civilian dress were spread out over a radius of five blocks. McMillan could sense an opportunity to get promoted and obliterating Emosemvi would certainly ensure it happened; he was among all the police officers from the Happiness City station right there at Erme's main entrance. His superiors had thought such a show of force to be excessive because ultimately the men from Emosemvi were few and poorly armed, however McMillan was not of the same mind and wanted to be sure to rout the resistance organization once and for all.

As the van headed towards Erme, it was spotted by a woman with a baby carriage, she pulled a cell phone out of her pocket and called McMillan to tell him that everything was going according to plan and in a few minutes the resistance people would get to him. McMillan gave the order to his men to load their rifles and fire at the van as soon as it was within range, and no one inside should be left alive.

In turn Romance suggested to his comrades they get the weapons out because they would soon be there.

William told Romance to stop the van next at a garage, then, to everyone's amazement, he ordered the group to get out without asking questions. Parked at the entrance to the garage was a red van belonging to the cleaning company Aegi. William told the group to load the gear into it and put on the red jumpsuits that were stowed in the back. Beatrice had a million questions, but she decided to remain silent, not knowing exactly what was going on.

The red van took off, burning rubber, and after taking several secondary roads so as not to attract too much attention, it reached the staff entrance to Happiness City police station. The security barrier opened automatically because an optical reader recognized the van's license plates, and the guard at the entrance gestured to William to enter, he waved at him and drove towards the underground parking lot. The Happiness City police station was deserted because all the available men were at the Erme national television center. The red van entered the garage, the group got out and with their guns at the ready walked towards an armored door.

William passed through the card reader a magnetic access badge showing the photo of Tim, their recently deceased friend who had worked there in the past. The door opened and the group went swiftly up a flight of steps, then William ordered everyone to put their guns inside a black plastic bag attached to a cleaning cart, so as not to attract the attention of the few policemen still in the building. Despite this ruse, a cop became suspicious and asked them to stop, the group began to run down the corridor, but it was a dead end with a locked armored door at the end. Meanwhile the cop had pulled out his pistol and was radioing for reinforcements. Beatrice was terrified and had seen the emotion of fear gradually appear on her friends' faces. "Will Emosemvi end its glorious existence in a dead end at a police station?" she wondered.

Romance pulled a rifle out of the black plastic bag and prepared to shoot, but William asked him to put it back. His friend did so although he was terrified and couldn't understand what was going on. Meantime the cop had got closer to them and by pointing his pistol was intimating that they surrender. William pushed the cleaning cart towards the cop, and he quickly glanced into the black plastic bag and saw the guns.

Everything seemed to be over, Orpheus stared at William hoping that he had a secret weapon or that he would do something unexpected to get them out of the situation, but nothing of the sort happened.

Jack could not believe that Virgilio's son himself had delivered them into the hands of the police. He would have followed him to the ends of the earth, but in that moment, he was confused and didn't know what to think. Another two policemen arrived, William put up no resistance even when one of them put a pair of handcuffs on him.

When every hope of escape seemed to have disappeared, the armored door behind the group opened wide and Stan, Tobias, James and Willy came out, rifles at the ready. In a flash, the members of the resistance vanished through the door, William energetically pushed his shoulder against the cop who had just handcuffed him, obliging him to come into the room too, while Romance closed the armored door behind them. It all happened so quickly that the cops didn't have time to react. The BT, J and O groups were inside the television recording room used by the police to broadcast messages to the population in the case of a natural disaster or other emergency. William knew the room because earlier, on his first day at work, Stuart had given him a tour of the station.

The cop unlocked the handcuffs at his wrists and with a conspiratorial look at William he exclaimed, "That was close!"

"Thanks Michael! Without your help we'd never have done it."

"I would do anything to avenge the death of my uncle. When you're ready, we can start," said the cop.

"All right, sit down in front of the television camera, and in a bit, we'll go on air."

Shots were heard coming from the corridor and Michael said, "My colleagues are shooting at the door lock to get through, but it's armored and will keep them out for a while."

As his friends were confused William felt he should explain what was going on. "My friends, when we had the meeting at the Bringlux, I already knew that I had a bug hidden in my coat. I don't know how long it had been there, but the important thing was finding it. So in the boiler room, for security reasons, I couldn't reveal my real plan entirely, but I instructed some of you separately. The mission entrusted to the BT group was a decoy, there was no flyer to print and distribute at the university and none of them would ever have had to go to the power station at Sadness City to deactivate the city's electricity. The aim was precisely to get them caught on the Elpis by the police force in order to get into a cell in this police station. Only Stan knew what the real plan was. Just before leaving the hotel I had given him the master key to open the cell where he and his group would be confined. I got hold of the key a while ago, when one evening I worked late here at the station. Stan knew exactly what time he had to escape from the cell to get to the television room and open the armored door."

Maggie couldn't hold back her astonishment and exclaimed, "Ingenious!"

"And that's not all," William replied, adding, "Before the J group left the Bringlux I asked Tim to give me his badge, thanks to which we managed to get into the building through the garage. At the end of our meeting in the boiler room, I wrote what Tim had to do on a piece of paper. He worked for the cleaning company Aegi and would have no problem getting hold of a red van and parking it in the garage where we found it. We went there in the white van so as to make McMillan believe we really did mean to go to Erme, the national television center at Sadness City. By means of the bug hidden in my coat, he had listened to our conversation in the boiler room and he was convinced that he would catch us red-handed at Erme, so he deployed all his men there, emptying the station at Happiness City. No one expected us to take on the police on their own ground and the factor of surprise was crucial for the success of the operation."

Everyone there was listening to the plan cleverly laid by William, and in their eyes, he was the hope of realizing the Emosemvi dream. It was as if, through his son, Virgilio was taking the resistance in hand and leading it to victory.

William went on without delay, "The J group's mission at the hydropower plant at Fear City was to stop Em 0 being mixed with the water. I had planned with Tim, but something went wrong and sadly he is dead. We had agreed they would place explosives outside the hydropower plant to blow it up as it had to be a quick and risk-free mission. Tim thought that some maintenance technicians were still in the building, so to save their lives he decided to go ahead to the plant control room, where he was caught along with Maggie and Seamus.

William pointed to the policeman and ended, "Lastly, Michael's help has been essential. He is the son of Castor, a very fine man I met in Africa whose brother was unfortunately killed by MC. Michael was with McMillan when the BT group was arrested on the Elpis and persuaded him to deploy all his men outside the Erme studios. Not only did Michael give the keys to this room to the BT group, he also brought an electricity generator here. No doubt when MC realizes what we are broadcasting on television, it will cut the electricity of the entire police station. Now my friends, let's go on air!"

Jack turned on the television camera positioned on a tripod right in front of William, who addressed the viewers,

"Good evening, my name is William, and I am the son of Virgilio Pattern, who was brutally killed by the men from Minedal-e Corporation. We are broadcasting this message from the television recording room at the police station of Happiness City, which we have seized.

We are the last bastion of the resistance. Don't believe the lies they tell you about us because the truth is that we haven't killed anyone. We only want to give back to all human beings what was taken away from them some time ago by Dr. Paul Shelton Malthen. It was he who spread the powerful Coris-91 virus on earth that decimated the population of the world, killing billions of people; then to be heralded as a hero and consolidate his financial empire, he developed a vaccine to which he mixed Em 0.

The camera tightened the shot to emphasize this key moment, while William got ready to continue his explanation, "The Em 0 is able to inhibit emotions and, in some cases, even erase the memories tied to them. In short, every human being can experience emotions, but they are inhibited by Em 0, which is not only injected at birth in every newborn but also spread through the water system. To bring an end to these crimes against humanity, we have halted the mixing process of Em 0 into the water at the hydropower plant at Fear City. At this very moment some of you can already experience vague emotions, although not intense. It may seem strange at first, and you'll feel a series of new sensations. Do not be alarmed because you are not showing the symptoms of an illness, you are getting better!"

At that moment, many people were tuned in to the television channel on which William was broadcasting his message. Some had already gone to the hospital precisely because as they were no longer taking in Em 0 with the water, they felt different and feared they were sick. At the emergency room there was a television and the people in the waiting room were listening to the resistance's message: they couldn't believe their eyes, and they stood as if petrified looking at the screen.

Romance pulled a vial of Reversing out of his pocket and passed it to William who continued his speech. "This is Reversing, and it totally nullifies the effects of Em 0. We are going to administer it to a volunteer to show you how it works. Then it is up to you to decide whether human beings deserve to experience emotions or not."

Using a syringe, William injected Reversing into Michael's neck. He began to move the muscles of his face in an uncontrolled manner, taking a few seconds to relax again. William showed the television camera a photo of a boyfriend and girlfriend as they happily hugged each other, then he turned to Michael asking, "What do you see?"

"I see two people hugging each other."

"Good, now close your eyes and think of the moment the gazes of the two lovers first met and when they exchanged true promises of love."

In the meantime, many viewers watching live from home or in public places also closed their eyes and began to imagine the scene of the two lovers.

William went on, "Imagine them smiling when their fingers touch for the first time, she blushes slightly because she is excited, while both their hearts beat to the rhythm of their love. It is neither too fast nor too slow, but exactly at the speed it should go. Then our two lovers kiss passionately, and, in a few years, they will know the joy of being parents."

Michael seemed very focused and wasn't missing a single word of that speech.

"We can also imagine the first meeting between a mother and her baby boy at the moment of birth. While the hospital room vanishes as if by magic, the mother with all her natural sensitivity and warmth welcomes the newborn who has lived in her for nine months, tenderly hugging him and lulling his cry with a smile and sweet words of gentleness. Grasping the poetry in every moment and appreciating the metaphor of life, knowing how to interpret it and live with passion, we will be able to perceive the sound of silence, the noise of a leaf falling, and the magic held in the gaze of our neighbor. Let's try to give value to little things because the sensitivity needed to turn them into great emotions is within reach and is often hidden in the creases of the faces of people close to us."

At that precise moment a smile appeared on Michael's face. Some viewers in turn managed to just make a faint smile, and they realized how much the leader of the pharmaceutical company Minedal-e had deceived them.

In the meantime McMillan had returned to the police station at Happiness City with his men and ordered the bomb disposal unit to blow up the armored door to the recording room where the members of the resistance were. The power was cut off inside the station, but the generator inside the television recording room automatically kicked in letting them continue broadcasting live.

William turned to Michael. "Now open your eyes. What is the name of the chief of police at Happiness City?"

"Richard McMillan."

William went on, "I would like to make something clear to viewers watching us at home. There are many honest people in the police force, but Chief of Police McMillan is not one of them. He works under cover for Minedal-e Corporation, to put it plainly: he is corrupt."

An expression of disgust appeared on Michael's face. William continued, "MC killed your uncle brutally, isn't that right?"

"Yes."

Sadness appeared on the policeman's face, then William pressed him, asking, "What do you feel for that pharmaceutical company?"

"I feel anger."

As Michael clenched his fists the expressions of anger and contempt appeared on his face. Then William stood before the television camera. "I will be honest with you. I do not think that every one of earth's inhabitants should necessarily be injected with Reversing, but I would like to give them the chance, and then everyone can choose freely what to do. Today I am also here to pay homage to the memory of my father, a man of steadfast ideals. He died to guarantee every one of you a future with a taste of freedom."

At this point tears flowed from his eyes and an expression of sadness appeared on his face. "Many of you will be asking yourselves what strange water is coming out of my eyes. They are called tears and are provoked by the emotion of sadness. It is not a pleasant experience but nonetheless it carries out a very important function in the precarious balance of our emotional states."

Then there was a loud explosion and the armored door to the television recording room blew up, a cloud of dust and debris hitting the members of the resistance. In a fraction of a second Michael's face and those of everyone present showed the expressions of surprise and fear. The police officers stormed into the room brandishing pistols and handcuffed the members of Emosemvi, who put up no resistance. The policemen were about to turn off the television camera, but still William managed a last word for the viewers, shouting, "We have shown you the other face of the world, now it is up to you to choose…"

A cop hit him in the face with a baton making him lose consciousness. Each member of the resistance was separated from the others and locked in a small cell to await interrogation by a judge. Doubtless they would all end up in prison to then be killed by MC operatives.

7.1

William had by now recovered his senses. McMillan was sitting in his cell and reading him his rights, then he moved closer to him and in a low voice told him to abandon all hope of survival because he would have him killed the following day. Night followed day and no one brought food or water to William, and at one point two cops entered his cell with batons and the intention of killing him.

McMillan showed up looking like someone who had won a hard battle and said, "The hydropower plant has been fixed and everything is back to normal. The newspapers and television channels are already harshly condemning your terrorist attack. World leaders are trying to drive out any other members of the resistance living abroad. In short: you have lost. Today Emosemvi died and with it your dreams of glory, prepare to meet your father!"

Just as moment when the cops were about to beat him to death with their batons, some shouts coming from the street attracted their attention. McMillan ordered his men to proceed to the police station entrance armed with automatic weapons. A crowd made up of thousands of people had forced its way through the checkpoint at the entrance of the station and was marching towards the main doors. The images shown the previous evening during the live broadcast had been around the world and the conscience of the people had been re-awoken as was slowly happening to their emotions.

In the police station entrance hall about forty officers were barricaded in riot gear and carrying automatic rifles. The crowd had almost reached the entrance to the station and some women carrying babies could also be seen. McMillan ordered his men to get ready to throw tear gas to disperse the crowd, and if that weren't enough any means at their disposition should be used to defend the building. He took his phone and called an unknown person, presumably his superior, asking what he should do. The unidentified man gave the order to shoot into the crowd to disperse it. By now the demonstrators were nearing the lobby, their faces did not seem to express any emotion, despite which they were one and all risking their lives for freedom.

McMillan ordered his men to load their rifles because at that point it would have been useless to use tear gas. The cops' index fingers lightly touched their triggers. The mothers with their children were at the front of the demonstrators and would be the first to die from the bullets. A woman with frizzy hair carrying a child of about two years of age was the first to enter the station hall. The cops felt no emotion and firing at the woman would not have caused them the least sadness for they had been trained to obey orders. That evening they would go home to their children and no one would ever blame them for the terrible actions committed against the demonstrators.

McMillan gave the order to fire, but what happened immediately afterwards changed the lives of billons of people and became part of the history of humanity.

Once they had received the order to fire from their boss, the policemen looked at each other, then they removed the magazines from their guns and put them on the ground. Despite not being able to feel emotions, they were not murderers and would not fire on unarmed people. McMillan became furious because he was losing control of the situation, he grabbed a rifle and prepared to shoot at the crowd, but a policeman took him by the collar of his uniform and threw him to the ground, then he handcuffed him and shut him in a cell.

The crowd freed William and his friends. The world changed radically that day, as if waking up from a long sleep. The Minedal-e Corporation headquarters at Disgust City were set on fire and all its laboratories around the world were converted into Reversing production centers. A few people on earth refused to inject themselves with the serum to regain their emotions, but the rest of the population of the world chose the road to freedom. Em 0 was eliminated from every hydropower plant and the statues of Paul Shelton Malthen disappeared from the face of the earth. McMillan, Peter and all the other men from MC were tried and sent to prison.

William chose to retire to the countryside with Beatrice to a farmhouse that belonged to old Tobias, whose land expropriated by the government in the past was returned to him. One evening they invited Stan, Tobias, James, Willy, Maggie, her husband Seamus, Jack and Romance to dinner. Orpheus had gone back to Africa because he couldn't get used to city life. That day Emosemvi, founded many years before by Virgilio, was dissolved by his son. Before saying goodbye to his friends William hugged them one by one, inviting them to come back and farm the land together.

The following week some journalists interviewed William, asking him if he was interested in transforming Emosemvi into a political party. He replied that the resistance was created for a precise purpose and once it had reached it there was no point in continuing a political struggle. The only thing to survive in time would be its story and the brotherly friendship of its members. Telling the Emosemvi story to future generations would keep alive the memory of what happened in the past so as not to make those mistakes again.

One day at sundown William and Beatrice went for a walk around the farmhouse. The silence of the evening was shyly embracing the world, then he gave her back the heart-shaped pendant, carefully guarded until that moment. Strangely the stars that evening were late appearing in the sky, as if, for a reason without logic, they had been hiding.

William held Beatrice tightly in his arms and in that precise moment she lit up all the stars in the night sky with the sparkle of her eyes.

THE END

Author's note

Important: as the following section reveals some plot details, I suggest you read to the end of the novel before reading this part.

At the start of the book, there is a reference to the River Lethe that is described both by Dante in the *Divine Comedy*,[1] and in the *Aeneid* by the Latin poet Virgil.[2] In mythology, it is considered the river of forgetfulness, where souls immerse themselves to be reincarnated and <u>forget</u> their past. In the novel, the river symbolically represents the lack of historical memory of the inhabitants of the various cities who only vaguely recall the old world, populated by people who were able to feel emotions.

As William is asleep in his apartment, he dreams of his grandfather Walter, who is holding a present and a card with the following message: "Happy Birthday from your friend Aesacus." Unwrapping the present William feels a strange tightening around his heart, it occurs to him that the feeling might be the slight hint of emotion. Then he rejects the possibility because it is clearly ridiculous. In the box there is a miniature ship, a small doll's cradle and a toy video camera. Aesacus is a figure from Greek mythology[3] with the gift of

---

[1] Alighieri D., *La Divina Commedia. Commento e parafrasi,* San Paolo Edizioni, 1998.
[2] Sermonti V., *L'Eneide di Virgilio*, BUR, 2008.
[3] Apollodoro, *Biblioteca,* G. Guidorizzi, J.G. Frazer, Biblioteca Adelphi, 1995.

interpreting dreams and predicting the future. The miniature ship refers to William's upcoming journey on a ship to Africa. The small doll's cradle alludes to maternity and in particular to William meeting his mother in the underground bunker. The toy video camera symbolically predicts what will happen inside the television recording room at the Happiness City police station from which Emosemvi broadcasts its message to the viewers.

In the video projected inside the old Eversten movie theater, William's father uses the following phrase: "Fate will find a way." This phrase is historically attributable to the supreme poet Publius Virgilius Maro, generally known as Virgil.

When William is taken to hospital after being nearly run over by a car, he meets a nurse called Hygieia. In mythology, Hygieia is the daughter of the god of medicine and is invoked to prevent illness. In classical art, Hygieia is shown in the act of letting a snake drink from a bowl. In the novel, William notices the nurse's tattoo of a bowl with a snake coiled around it.

At the Somtlose William meets a woman from the resistance by the name of Tisiphone; the men from MC have killed her mother and she is unjustly charged with the crime. In Greek mythology, Tisiphone has the task of punishing crimes against blood relatives such as patricide, matricide, fratricide and homicide. She is portrayed as a woman with snakes as hair and eyes of flame. In the novel, Tisiphone is described as a woman with green-tinted hair (the color of reptiles) with reddish eyes. On the back of her hand, she also has a tattoo of a snake with red eyes. What is more, she keeps her snake inside a basket with the Reversing. In Virgil's *Aeneid*[4] Tisiphone is described as one of the guardians of the gates of Tartarus. In Hesiod's *Theogony,*[5] in which the history and genealogy of the Greek gods are told, Tartarus is a murky underground place in which Zeus confines the Titans after defeating them. In the novel, Tartarus is the name of MC's underground bunker in Niger.

Tisiphone tells William that at the head of Minedal-e Corporation is a woman named Campe. Towards the end of the novel, it becomes clear that this is William's mother. In Greek mythology, Campe is the guardian of Tartarus, and her appearance is that of an old woman armed with two poisonous swords. In the novel, the symbol of Minedal-e Corporation is a triangle enclosed in a circle inside of which are two crossed swords beneath the initials "M" and "C."

The large ship on which William sails to Africa is a reference to the Greek myth of Pandora's box; a terracotta vase is painted on the ship's side with the name "Elpis." In mythology, Elpis is the spirit of hope, kept with other elements in the box that Zeus presents to Pandora. Legend has it that no evil then existed in the world and human

---

[4] Ibid.
[5] Esiodo, *Teogonia*, translation by. E. Romagnoli, BUR, 1984.

beings couldn't fall ill, much less grow old. Despite the fact that Zeus tells Pandora not to open the box he has given her, she disobeys him, and the evils escape that still today afflict the world, such as old age, pain, vice, jealousy, etc. Aware that all the things are escaping from the box, Pandora hurriedly closes it again, leaving inside only hope that did not escape in time. So the world knows chaos until Pandora decides to open the box again and allow hope to come out and bring balance to the earth once more.

The last name of John, William's colleague who betrays him in the novel, is Apate. In Greek mythology "Apate" is the deity of deceit and also one of the spirits contained in Pandora's box.

In Dakar, William meets a member of the resistance named Castor and his mother Leda. Castor tells William the story of his brother, a boxer killed by MC as he is returning from the gym. In Greek, Etruscan and Roman mythology Castor is a tamer of horses while his brother Pollux is a boxer, and both are sons of Leda and considered the protectors of sailors in stormy seas.

Castor advises William to go to dock 23 at dawn. There a truck with the symbol of a white shell with a cross on top painted on its sides picks him up. Since ancient times, the shell has been the symbol for a long journey because it is worn by pilgrims. In the past, particular shells known as scallops could only be found on a certain beach that was the destination of many pilgrimages; those who reached the beach would take a shell back to their hometown as proof that they had completed the journey.

In Africa, the truck driver is named Orpheus. After traveling all day in the direction of Niger, in the evening he stops near a forest. Orpheus begins to play his lyre and the melody coming from the instrument is so exquisite that it even quiets the noise of the animals in the nearby forest, as though the notes placate their souls by offering them peace. Soon the melody puts the world to sleep, lulling their dreams in the fragrance of life. Orpheus is a figure from Greek mythology capable of enchanting even wild animals with the sound of his lyre.

In a village not far from the MC bunker, William meets Tiresias. The man with an enigmatic face with <u>features that are very like those of a woman</u> has been <u>blinded</u> by the men from MC and seems to be able to predict the future. In ancient mythology, Tiresias is a famous Theban clairvoyant. Among the many legends, one recounts how one day Tiresias sees two snakes mating, so he hits the female, and, in a flash, he is turned into a woman, then after a few years, he wounds the male of the same couple of snakes and is transformed back into a man. Precisely because he has lived both <u>as a man and a woman,</u> the deities want to know from him whether it is the man or the woman who has the greatest pleasure in love. He replies that of the two, without a doubt it is the woman who has more pleasure. As his reply did not please the goddess Hera, she <u>blinds him,</u> while Zeus is pleased by the reply and rewards him by giving him the gift of seeing into the future.

When William meets his mother in the bunker, he realizes that the name of the pharmaceutical company Minedal-e is in fact an anagram of the name Madeline. The coordinates of the bunker Tartarus where William meets his mother are: 13°14'51.2"N 9°14'05.0"E. These coordinates are not made up, but really exist and correspond to a real place in Niger. Furthermore, each number and pair of numbers in the coordinates corresponds exactly to a letter in the English alphabet. The string of letters makes the name "Madeline." In other words, the first number of the code, 13, corresponds to the thirteenth letter of the alphabet, which is **M**, the number 1 stands for the letter **A**, 4 is **D**, while 5 is the letter **E**, 12 is **L**, the number 9 corresponds to the letter **I**, 14 to the letter **N** and number 5 to **E**. So William's mother's name is hidden within the coordinates.

Bringlux is both the name of the hotel and of its owner and can be translated as "Light bringer." The funnel shape of the Bringlux recalls hell, as described by Dante in the *Divine Comedy*.[6] Unlike Dante's *Inferno*, which is shaped like a funnel extending towards the center of the earth, the Bringlux has the shape of an upside down funnel, with the wide base placed on the land and the narrower end pointing up to the sky. The Bringlux has nine floors with a variable number of rooms. In the novel, the hotel's seventh floor

---

[6] Alighieri D., op. cit.

only has three large rooms, whereas the eighth has ten and the ninth floor has four.

The <u>nine</u> floors at the Bringlux represent the <u>nine</u> circles of hell as described by Dante. The <u>three</u> rooms on the <u>seventh</u> floor of the hotel correspond to the <u>three</u> rings in the <u>seventh</u> circle of hell in the *Divine Comedy*, while the <u>ten</u> rooms on the <u>eighth</u> floor of the hotel correspond to the <u>ten</u> evil ditches of Dante's *Inferno*, in the <u>eighth</u> circle. Finally, in the *Divine Comedy*, the <u>ninth</u> circle of hell, is divided into <u>four</u> rings just as the Bringlux hotel has <u>four</u> rooms on the <u>ninth</u> floor.

It is left to the imagination of the reader to figure out who the owner of the Bringlux really is. Hint: He is at the reception behind a transparent counter very like a large cube of ice in shape and luminosity.

The blond woman wearing a red dress with a low neckline at the reception of the Bringlux represents lust. She is complaining because in her room, on the <u>second floor</u>, the blast of the air conditioning is so strong that she can't even sleep. Addressing the receptionist the woman says, "That infernal blast of air nearly knocked me over, it's an absolute gale. I hope you can send someone up to repair it!" In Dante's *Inferno* he places the lustful in the <u>second circle</u>. There the law of *contrappasso* means that, precisely because during their earthly life they were overwhelmed by an unstoppable passion, in hell they are blown about in the air by an incessant infernal squall.

The guest in line behind the blond woman is a middle-aged man, noticeably overweight and wearing an orange robe. He has only just finished eating a snack and with chocolate around his mouth he tells the receptionist, "The carpet in my room is all muddy, and the shower is so cold that it's like icy rain." In this case too, the receptionist is very patient and obliging, moving the gentleman to another room also on the <u>third floor</u>. In Dante's *Inferno* the <u>third circle</u> is that of the gluttonous. They are immersed in a mire and tormented by an incessant downpour of snow and hail.

The third and last person the receptionist deals with tells a story that is verging on the incredible. He is dressed in the remains of a well-tailored suit that is now reduced to tatters and, although owning the hotel, he is saying that he has no money because he has spent it elsewhere, then he adds, "I was walking just outside the hotel when some dogs chased and mauled me, scratching my arms and ruining my suit. I hope you don't mind if I settle my account another time." The receptionist seems to understand fully the guest's distress and allows him to delay payment. He hands him the key to his room on the <u>seventh floor</u> and says goodbye with great cordiality. In the <u>seventh circle</u> of Dante's *Inferno* are the violent and in particular in the second ring the profligate who squandered their possessions during their lifetime. Their punishment is to be mauled by ferocious dogs.

The owner of the Bringlux hotel takes the members of the resistance to a large room where the walls are covered in white leather and a large crystal chandelier with incandescent light bulbs hangs from the ceiling, and on the floor, there is a large oriental carpet with the letter "Y" woven into the middle. Since the time of the Pythagorean school[7] the letter Y stands for a fork leading down two distinct paths to two opposites: vice and virtue. In Virgil's *Aeneid*,[8] through a forked golden bough very similar in shape to the letter Y, Aeneas manages to reach the underworld. The symbol represents the common origin of good and evil that separate and take different paths.

In the room where Bringlux takes the members of the resistance, there is no furniture, only a clear case to keep the dust from the crystal glasses and a wooden cup inside. The smell of incense fills the air although there is no sign of an aroma diffuser.

Bringlux holds his face a few inches from a minuscule retinal scanner then out of the wall comes a small keyboard, and he keys in the code: "2522Y." The walls of the room flip over, turning back to front and revealing to those present a rack with an orderly display of various automatic guns and other gear. The code tapped in by Bringlux on the little keyboard has a specific meaning. The letter Y is the twenty-fifth letter of the modern Latin alphabet, while it is the twenty-second of the ancient Latin one, hence the code "2522Y."

The novel has many other symbolic elements, as well as historical and film references which are intentionally not

---

[7] Christiane L., *Pitagora e il suo influsso sul pensiero e sull'arte*, Italian translation by P. Faccia, Akeios, 2008.
[8] Sermonti V., op. cit.

mentioned here to let the readers discover them as they read.

Author biography

Emiliano Forino Procacci is a psychotherapist who specializes in verbal and nonverbal communication and in encoding /decoding facial expression. After being awarded two master's degrees, he continued his training in London and California.

He has invented an innovative method for selecting personnel based on assessment techniques, reading facial micro-expressions and body language.

He is the author of several books and owner of the trademark Unstatus Luxury™.

Instagram: emiliano_forino_procacci

Facebook: Emiliano Forino Procacci

Bibliography

Alighieri D., *La Divina Commedia. Commento e parafrasi,* San Paolo Edizioni, 1998.

Apollodoro, *Biblioteca,* G. Guidorizzi, J.G. Frazer, Biblioteca Adelphi, 1995.

Christiane L., *Pitagora e il suo influsso sul pensiero e sull'arte,* Italian translation by P. Faccia, Akeios,2008.

Esiodo, *Teogonia,* translation. by E. Romagnoli, BUR, 1984.

Sermonti V., *L'Eneide di Virgilio,* BUR, 2008.

Enjoy other books by Emiliano Forino Procacci

A WORLD WITHOUT EMOTIONS: EVOLUTION

(2020) – Italian and English version – Third place at the

Book Fest Awards 2022.

Ancient symbols and myths form the backdrop to an action-packed, twisting storyline in which William Pattern has to solve complicated puzzles to restore world order.

The protagonist goes in search of a truth buried among the monuments of a city rich in history, so that the love of truth may triumph. Guided by his instinct, he must discover what lies behind an ancient legend and mysterious Latin inscriptions.

A surreal atmosphere envelops a world in which human beings have lost their emotions and everyone wears neutral facial expressions.

This thrilling tale is the setting of a love story between two human beings made to fight for their dream of living a happy life together.

A WORLD WITHOUT EMOTIONS: THE PATH OF LIGHT (2021) – Available in Italian and soon in English.

THE SUPERHERO OF EMOTION – (2022) -
Available in Italian and soon in English.

A superhero, a secret organization that wants to subvert the world order and a mysterious red stone. These are just some elements of the new novel by Emiliano Forino Procacci which presents for the first time in the world an exceptional character with the ability to govern emotions.

Historical elements, action, love stories and enigmas are the background to an original plot full of twists and turns.

You can be a superhero every day by helping others, exercising willpower and calling on inner resources.
Nihil difficult volenti: nothing is difficult for the one who wants.

THE COMMUNICATION LIVES IN THE PAST - Genealogy of an ancient European family (2017) - Available in Italian and soon in English.